ONE FOR EACH NIGHT

THE GREATEST
CHANUKAH STORIES
OF ALL TIME

NEW VESSEL PRESS
NEW YORK

 New Vessel Press

www.newvesselpress.com

Library of Congress Cataloging-in-Publication Data

Various
One for Each Night: The Greatest Chanukah Stories of All Time / various authors.
p. cm.
ISBN 978-1-954404-22-9
Library of Congress Control Number 2023931439
Chanukah—Fiction

Table of Contents

✡   ✡   ✡   ✡   ✡

ONE FOR EACH NIGHT

A Chanukah Tale from Old Russia

Curt Leviant

This is the story my father, Ya'akov, told me. He had heard it from his grandfather, Chaim, who was a young man in the Russian shtetl when the event took place, during the mid-1800s.

Early one morning, one snowless winter's day, end of November, just before Chanukah, a solidly built man—he seemed to be in his mid-thirties—appeared in our shtetl, Kariukovke. He wore a khaki-colored greatcoat, a peasant's hat with earflaps, and he had a knapsack on his back. It was obviously an army uniform but it lacked any insignias or markings. He spoke a rough-edged Yiddish with an equally rough Russian accent.

People noticed him when they came out of shul. But since he wore a uniform people hesitated to approach him, their reticence to have contact with the czarist authority ingrained in them. But he didn't look like an official at all. In fact, he looked like a lost soul. To the first groups of Jews he met, he said he had just finished his obligatory twenty-five years of service in the czar's army and he was returning home. He said his name was Dovid.

Judging by the way he spoke, people looked at him skeptically.

"Are you a Jew?"

He laughed bitterly. "What? You think I'm a goy? In the army they sure didn't treat me like a goy. *Ikh bin a Yid*," he added in Yiddish. "I am a Jew."

But people weren't convinced. Out of range of his hearing, they murmured that he was a Russki trying to get money before Chanukah, or perhaps find lodging in the old age home, which always welcomed Jewish travelers.

"Why did you come to Kariukovke?"

"Where else should I go? This is where I was born, where my family lived, and it is from here the czar's abductors took me to the army. I was not yet thirteen."

It was true, I thought. Years ago, the abductors, "snatchers," *khappers* they were called in Yiddish, were active, taking even little children. But Kariukovke had suffered a rare pogrom about a dozen years back and many Jews left the shtetl. Other Jews, fleeing incidents in their villages, sought refuge in Kariukovke. Jews evidently put into practice the old Hebrew expression: Change your place, change your luck. In any case, no one in town remembered such an abduction from twenty-five years ago. Indeed, throughout the years some youngsters left of their own accord to try their luck in America.

"Take me to my father Motl's house."

"Motl who? There are and there were lots of Motls here."

"Motl the carpenter."

I saw the men looking at one another. One of them, the oldest of the group, a man in his seventies, nodded his head slowly.

"There actually were three by that name. But none are alive."

"None? Not one? My father dead?"

"We had a pogrom here about twelve years ago, which you obviously didn't know about. And people die just like that too."

The newcomer, who said his name was Dovid, covered his face with his hands and began sobbing like a baby.

"And what's your mother's name?"

"Rivke."

"Do you know how many Rivkes we have here?"

"But married to Motl the carpenter?"

The men looked at one another and shrugged.

"What's your family name?"

"We hardly ever used our family name," Dovid said. "They called my father Motl the carpenter and I was Motl's son. And in the army they didn't use last names. They always called me Motl Yid."

"Wait a minute," the older man said. "Now I remember. There was a Rivke married to a Motl the carpenter. I think the family name was Shatsky."

"Dovid, was your family name Shatsky?" I asked.

"Maybe."

"What do you mean, maybe. How can a man forget his family name?"

"Like I said, they never called you by your family name. Anyway, do we use family names here in the shtetl? You're called by your first name and what line of work you do. Like Motl *shneider*, the tailor. And Avrom *shuster*, the shoemaker. And if you've been in the czar's army for twenty-five years, and your childhood and youth and many of your precious grown-up years are wasted, you forget a lot of things. It's a miracle I remember what I remember."

All the people around me stared at him. He looked like a goy but spoke Yiddish. He threw in lots of Russian words, and at times it seemed he was translating from Russian into Yiddish. Had you heard him from a distance his language would not have sounded Yiddish. His speech had the rhythms and cadences of Russian. And it should be said that speaking Yiddish did not automatically identify a person as a Jew. We had a number of goyim in town who worked for Jews who spoke Yiddish fluently.

The ex-soldier, Dovid, claimed that he had spoken only Russian for twenty-five years. That was probably why the Slavic overwhelmed his Yiddish.

Then someone in our group took out a little siddur and showed it to Dovid. "Can you read?"

"I haven't looked at a siddur in twenty-five years. I forgot how to read."

"How can a Jew forget to read?"

Dovid came up to the man and looked him in the face. The man, apparently frightened, backed off.

"Have you ever been in the czar's army for twenty-five years? Anything, everything, is possible . . . But I still remember the Shma Yisroel. That they couldn't wipe away from me. I said it to myself every night. Every night. I didn't miss a night." And he brought the palm of his right hand to his eyes, covered them, and recited the Shma fervently.

But even this did not persuade the group of grown-ups near me. I heard them saying that they had known Russkies who could imitate those words and that gesture too.

But why should a Russian want to pass himself off as a Jew in a land where there was lots of anti-Semitism, both popular and official? The answer is that the Jewish community was known for caring for its own.

The man who claimed to be Dovid was no doubt hoping for a bed in the poorhouse or in the old age home, or a place in someone's house until he found a job. He was still a young man and would likely find work as a carpenter.

"*Ikh bin a Yid*," he kept saying, at times declaring it forthrightly, at times in a tone of complaint. "They snatched me away when I was only twelve, a year before my bar mitzvah, and forced me into the army. They wanted to break me, all the anti-Semites, but they didn't. They couldn't make me a Christian. I'm still a Jew. *Ikh bin a Yid*."

The men speaking to him exchanged glances. He was sounding more and more like a Jew. But what Jew didn't know his family name? What Jew can't read from the siddur? What Jew has the gruff look of a goy? And what Jew speaks Yiddish like it comes out of the mouth of a *muzhik*, a peasant?

Because of the turmoil that Kariukovke had experienced, and because Dovid's parents were no longer alive, there was no one who could remember his kidnapping into the czar's army.

"I was looking for my father's little house before I met you," Dovid told us. "But I couldn't find it. The town has changed."

"We've had turmoil here," one of the men near me said. "Pogroms. Fires. New construction ordered by the authorities."

Dovid looked down. "I thought I would be able to return to my parents' house."

We didn't know what to say. I felt sorry for the man. Should I invite him to stay with our family?

Meanwhile, Dovid stood there silently, shifting his weight from one leg to another.

One of the men near me ran into a house and came out with a glass of water for Dovid, which he drank eagerly.

"Are you hungry?" another man asked.

Dovid shook his head. Then he said in an upbeat voice, "Is Avrom the teacher still alive?"

We looked at him, bewildered. How did he know the old teacher?

"Why do you ask?"

"Is he alive?"

"Yes, he's very old."

"I know. He wasn't young years ago. Where is he?"

"Why do you want to know?"

"Why don't you answer me? Stop asking me why. Where does he live?"

"In the old age home."

"Is he well?"

"For a man in his late eighties, maybe nineties, he is quite well and alert."

"Take me to him. I want to see him."

We all walked through the quiet streets to the two-story community old age home. Inside a few residents sat in the living room.

We walked up to Reb Avrom's room, knocked on the door, and opened it. Reb Avrom was sitting at his table, studying a text. He was no doubt surprised to see so many people, including one who looked like a soldier. Avrom was a short, thin man, with a wispy white beard and a black yarmulke on his head. He looked calmly at all of us, but stared intently at the ex-soldier.

As soon as Dovid saw the old man he ran up to him and cried out, his voice choking, "Rebbe, it's me, your student, Dovid. Do you remember me?"

Avrom rose, and with an agility that belied his years, he gave us that heartfelt broad smile that was an ingrained part of his personality.

"Dovid. Dovid." Avrom shook his head, a sort of rocking motion that did not quite indicate yes or no.

"Rebbe, you were my teacher. I was twelve years old. Studying with you. It was a few days before Chanukah, just like right now, when the czar's men came in suddenly and snatched me away."

"How many years ago?"

"Twenty-five."

Now Reb Avrom was nodding. "Yes. It sounds familiar. A long time ago."

"Twenty-five years, Rebbe," Dovid said with a tear in his voice. "Twenty-five long years with them. They tried, but they couldn't break me. *Ikh bin a Yid. Ikh bin geblibn a Yid.* I remained a Jew."

Reb Avrom clapped his hands and cried out, "They burst in. I pleaded with them. He's an only child, I said. It's against the czar's law to take an only child.

☆ 5 ☆

But they didn't listen. They didn't care. They got paid for snatching. I remember It was a cold day. A few days before Chanukah."

And Dovid added: "I asked the soldiers, let me at least say goodbye to my father and mother. But they didn't. They didn't let me." Here Dovid's voice broke. "They took me away."

Now the ex-soldier's eyes widened and a glow spread over his dusky face as if he was having a revelation. He looked at Reb Avrom's face as though he wanted to absorb its essence.

"Rebbe, we were studying the laws of Chanukah when they barged in."

Reb Avrom interrupted. "Yes, yes. That's what I was going over with you. From Joseph Caro's the *Shulchan Aruch*, the Code of Law."

"You were reading what happens if a person doesn't have enough money to buy both Shabbes candles and Chanukah candles."

Reb Avrom began in a singsong voice, reciting in Hebrew. "It's from Chapter 678 from the *Shulchan Aruch*. If one has insufficient means to purchase both Chanukah candles and Shabbes candles . . ."

Dovid closed his eyes and continued chanting in Hebrew with his rebbe. Now both their voices rang out and, as if in a rehearsed duet, their two voices joined in song:

". . . that person should purchase Shabbes candles because they bring about peace in one's household."

Then the teacher fell silent and the czar's soldier continued chanting alone, remembering the words of the *Shulchan Aruch*:

"But If one already owns Shabbes candles but only has enough money to either purchase wine for the Shabbes kiddush or Chanukah candles, then one should purchase Chanukah candles since it involves showing off the miracle of Chanukah."

With tears in his eyes, Reb Avrom came up to Dovid, embraced him and kissed both his cheeks. The tears of both men intermingled.

"That's what we were studying when they came . . . And you remembered every word. After twenty-five years."

"Dear Rebbe. I always thought of you. You were like a second father to me."

And Dovid bent down and kissed his rebbe's cheek.

"*Borukh ha-bo, tayerer Yid*. Welcome, dear Jew. Welcome home. And a *freylekhen Hanuka*. A happy Chanukah to you."

I looked around. Every man's face was wet; yet every man was smiling. Now all of us also embraced Dovid. And now we all vied as to who would be the first to welcome him and stay with us throughout Chanukah until he settled in.

And with the return of a Jew to our shtetl after twenty-five years, it was indeed a *freylekhen* Chanukah in Kariukovke.

2020

To Grandpa's House for Latkes

Leon Elbe

"Tonight, my son, you have to go to bed early because tomorrow night is the third candle. We're going to Grandpa's house for latkes and we'll be celebrating until late at night."

That's what Mama said to Yingele-Ringele, the boy with the magic ring. The boy already knew what the "third candle" meant. He knew that when it's Chanukah, you have to bless the Chanukah candles, starting with a single candle and then lighting one more each night, and so on and so forth for a full eight nights until the holiday ends and Chanukah is over. Each night of the holiday is counted by its candles: the first night is the first candle, the second night is the second candle, and the third night is the third candle, and on and on. And for the third candle, as the boy knows, his family always goes to Grandpa's house to have latkes. It's been that way every year since he can remember. Grandpa gives him a dreidel made of lead, and he spins it, as happy as a king in his castle. Grandma brings hot latkes to the table and Grandpa tells Chanukah stories, such wonderful stories!

And so when Yingele-Ringele—the boy with the magic ring—heard that tomorrow night was the third candle and they would once again be going to Grandpa's to have latkes, he started dancing and jumping, and burst into a little song:

Mama, Mama, Maminkah!
It's Chan-a, Chan-a, Chanukah!

A lot, a lot of latkes,
so greasy and so fine
We will spin the dreidel
and have the best of times
I spin my little toy
Chanukah brings such joy!

Then the boy said good night to his mother and said good night to his father and fell fast asleep.

And as he slept, he sleepily remembered that he really did need to go see the king in his castle on the other side of the river and meet the prince and the princess there. He was walking and walking along the path when his grandfather appeared right in front from him.

"And where are you going?" Grandpa asked.

"I am going to see the king in his castle," the boy replied.

"But you won't come to me for latkes?" Grandpa asked. "It's Chanukah after all, the third candle!"

"No, Zeyde. Before all that, I need to go see the king," the boy replied. "I've been walking and walking for such a long time, but I still haven't made it there. They say that everything is so beautiful and happy in the castle!"

The boy wanted to leave, but his grandfather stopped him. "Wait a minute! Before you go, I want to tell you a story about a king. You'll see—faced with his crown, you'd surely frown!"

And so Grandpa began his tale:

Once upon a time there was a king,
a man who did many wicked things.
"Beat the Jews!" he screamed and swore.
The people cried, "We cannot take this any more!"
Although his list of horrors is quite ample,
I'll give you here just one example:
Once, he tore the tongue out from a youth—
It's terrible, but it's the truth!
What did the child do to deserve such a thing?

He would not bow, nor kiss the king's ring!
That ring—not like the golden band
that shines so nicely on your hand—
would only make the blackest magic
The results of which were just so tragic
"Beat the Jews!" he screamed and swore.
The people cried, "We cannot take this any more!"

Then one man stood up brave and tall:
"Down with the king! He must fall!
If he beats us, then we'll beat him too
Freedom for all, justice for the Jews!"
The people agreed: "Take him down!"
But the soldiers were loyal to the crown.
A war began: an army against the masses
The Jews united against the ruling classes
They fought hard and came out ahead
The battle was won and the king was dead!

The Jews rejoiced, at last rid of their horrible ruler.
In honor of their victory they created the holiday of Chanukah
and lit candles in celebration.
No more crowns, no more frowns!

As Grandpa told his story, the boy with the magic ring stood and listened. When the story was finished, Grandpa said, "You see what happened once upon a time with a king? I'm worried that your king won't be any better. Don't spend your time with him! Better you should come to my house to have some latkes. I'll give you a dreidel too."

"You're right, Zeyde," answered the boy. "I'll go with you."

They took to the path. But suddenly, it started to snow and it snowed so hard that they could no longer see where they were going. The boy cried out, "Zeyde! Snow is blocking the path!"

"Nothing to worry about!" Grandpa said. "Let it fall! The path is big and wide enough for all. Let's go, all three of us together—you, me, and the snow in between! It's always so nice when it snows on Chanukah. Another reason to celebrate!"

They continued walking and walking. The snow was getting deeper and deeper and it was almost impossible to keep going.

"Hush now!" said Grandpa to the boy. "You're Yingele-Ringele, the boy with the magic ring, a ring that can do anything! Make a wish and ask for a sleigh!"

"Yes, Zeyde, of course!" said the boy. "That's just what I'll do." The boy spoke into his magic ring:

Right away from far or near
Let a magic sleigh appear!

As soon as the boy uttered these words, there appeared a sleigh, drawn by three horses nimble as deer and strong as lions.

The boy mounted the sleigh together with his grandfather and the sleigh flew through snow and storm as fast as an arrow darting from a bow until it arrived at the spot where Grandpa's house should have stood.

Grandpa looked everywhere for his house, searching and searching, but couldn't find it anywhere. So much snow had fallen that Grandpa's house was completely buried. Not even the chimney top could be seen.

"Hush now!" said Grandpa to the boy. "You've got the magic ring! Make a wish and tell it to uncover the house!"

The boy spoke into the magic ring:

Ring of magic, make it so
Dig Grandpa's house out from under the snow!

And the magic ring did just that. Soon the house stood before them, cleared of the snow. Grandpa and the boy went inside and together they celebrated the holiday until the morning.

1929

The Menorah

Theodor Herzl

Once there was a man who deep in his soul felt the need to be a Jew. His material circumstances were satisfactory enough. He was making an adequate living and was fortunate to have a vocation in which he could create according to the impulses of his heart. You see, he was an artist. He had long ceased to trouble his head about his Jewish origin or the faith of his fathers, when the age-old hatred reasserted itself under a fashionable slogan. Like many others, our man, too, believed that this movement would soon subside. But instead of getting better, it got worse. Although he was not personally affected by them, the attacks pained him anew each time. Gradually his soul became one bleeding wound.

This secret psychic torment had the effect of steering him to its source, namely, his Jewishness, with the result that he experienced a change that he might never have had in better days, because he had become so alienated: He began to love Judaism with great fervor. At first he did not fully acknowledge this mysterious affection, but finally it grew so powerful that his vague feelings crystallized into a clear idea to which he gave voice: the thought that there was only one way out of this Jewish suffering—namely, to return to Judaism.

When his best friends, whose situation was similar to his, found out about this, they shook their heads and thought he had gone out of his mind. How could something that only meant an intensification and deepening of the malady be a remedy? He, on the other hand, thought that the moral distress of modern Jews was so acute because they had lost the spiritual counterpoise which our strong forefathers had possessed. People ridiculed him behind his back. Some even laughed right in his face. But he did not let the silly remarks of people whose judgment he had never before had occasion to value throw him off his course, and he bore their malicious or good-natured jests with equanimity. And since his behavior was not otherwise irrational, people eventually left him to his whim, although some used a stronger term, *idée fixe*, to describe it.

In his patient way, our man displayed the courage of his conviction over and over again. There were a number of changes which he himself found hard to accept, although he was stubborn enough not to let on. As a man and an artist of modern sensibilities, he was deeply rooted in many non-Jewish customs, and he had absorbed ineradicable elements from the cultures of the nations among which his intellectual pursuits had taken him. How was this to be reconciled with his return to Judaism? This gave rise to many doubts in his own mind about the soundness of his guiding idea, his *idée maitresse*, as a French thinker has called it. Perhaps the generation that had grown up under the influence of other cultures was no longer capable of that return which he had discovered as the solution. But the next generation, provided it was given the right guidance early enough, would be able to do so. He therefore tried to make sure that his own children, at least, would be shown the right way. He was going to give them a Jewish education from the very beginning.

In previous years he had let the festival which for centuries had illuminated the marvel of the Maccabees with the glow of candles pass by unobserved. Now, however, he used it as an occasion to provide his children with a beautiful memory for the future. An attachment to the ancient nation was to be instilled early in these young souls. A menorah was acquired, and when he held this nine-branched candelabrum in his hands for the first time, a strange mood came over him. In his remote youth, in his father's house, such little lights had burned and there was something intimate and homelike about the holiday. This tradition did not seem chill or dead. The custom of kindling one light with another had been passed on through the ages.

The ancient form of the menorah also gave him food for thought. When had the primitive structure of this candelabrum first been devised? Obviously, its form had originally been derived from that of a tree: The sturdy stem in the center; four branches to the right and four to the left, each below the other, each pair on the same level, yet all reaching the same height. A later symbolism added a ninth, shorter branch which jutted out in front and was called the *shamash* or servant. With what mystery had this simple artistic form, taken from nature, been endowed by successive generations? And our friend, who was, after all, an artist, wondered whether it would not be possible to infuse new life into the rigid form of the menorah, to water its roots like those of a tree. The very sound of the name, which he now pronounced in front of his children every evening, gave him pleasure. Its sound was especially lovely when it came from the mouth of a child.

The first candle was lit and the origin of the holiday was retold: the miracle of the little lamp which had burned so much longer than expected, as well as the story of the return from the Babylonian exile, of the Second Temple, of the Maccabees. Our friend told his children all he knew. It was not much but for them it was enough. When the second candle was lit, they repeated what he had told them. And although they had learned it all from him, it seemed to him quite new and beautiful. In the days that followed he could hardly wait for the evenings, which became ever brighter. Candle after candle was lit in the menorah, and together with his children, the father mused upon the little lights. At length his reveries became more than he could or would tell them, for his dreams would have been beyond their understanding.

When he had resolved to return to the ancient fold and openly acknowledge his return, he had only intended to do what he considered honorable and sensible. But he had never dreamed that on his way back home he would also find gratification for his longing for beauty. Yet what befell him was nothing less. The menorah with its growing brilliance was indeed a thing of beauty, and inspired lofty thoughts. So he set to work and with an expert hand sketched a design for a menorah to present to his children the following year. He made a free adaption of the motif of the eight arms of equal height which projected from the central stem to the right and to the left, each pair on the same level. He did not consider himself bound by the rigid traditional form, but created again directly from nature, unconcerned with other interpretations which, of course, continued to be no less valid on that account. What he was aiming for was vibrant beauty. But even as he brought new motion into the rigid forms, he still observed their tradition, the refined old style of their arrangement. It was a tree with slender branches, whose ends opened up like calyxes, and it was these calyxes that were to hold the candles.

With such thoughtful occupation the week passed. There came the eighth day, on which the entire row of lights is kindled, including the faithful ninth candle, the shamash, which otherwise only serves to light the others. A great radiance shone forth from the menorah. The eyes of the children sparkled. For our friend, the occasion became a parable for the awakening of a whole nation. First one candle—it is still dark and the solitary light looks gloomy. Then it finds a companion, then another, and yet another. The darkness must retreat. The young and the poor are the first to see the light. Then the others join in, all those who love justice, truth, liberty, progress, humanity and beauty. When all the candles are ablaze everyone must stop in amazement and rejoice at what has been wrought. And no office is more blessed than that of a servant of this light.

1897

What's the Meaning of Chanukah?

Mendele Moykher-Sforim

"A great miracle happened to me on Chanukah."

"What do you mean 'to you,' Shmuel? How about 'to us'? Isn't it as much my miracle as yours?"

"Actually, dear Ignatz, a great miracle happened to *me* on Chanukah—to *me* and not to you."

"What's the point of arguing with a *beys-medresh* old-timer? As far as you're concerned, we, today's Jews, aren't Jews at all, and you house-of-study bookworms from the olden days have some kind of contract with the Master of the Universe, an exclusive claim to *yidishkeyt*."

"Nothing you're saying, Ignatz, is in the least connected to the story that I mean to tell you. By the way, today's not the right moment for such quarrels. We have better things to do—throw together a card game, eat latkes, and spend time with the crowd. That's why I invited you over, my good fellow—but seeing as the other guests haven't arrived yet, and you brought up this touchy subject, well—I'll just have to give you a thorough answer. You understand, we're all Jews, whether observant or *maskilim*, God-fearing or secular. I, for example, 'dwelt in the tents of Shem' from earliest childhood, in *kheyder*, in *yeshive*, whereas you went to 'school' and didn't know the meaning of 'the yoke of Torah,' yet nevertheless we're both Jews. So what's the difference between us? *Yidishkeyt* engraved itself in my heart, in my mind, and in each of my two hundred and forty-eight limbs.

I, and those like me, have a special appreciation for Jewish custom—it's in our bones, whether we know it or not. Even if we stray, even if we convert—God forbid!—we'll never forget the feel of *yidishkeyt*. But when it comes to someone like you—someone who never 'immersed himself in Torah and devotion,' a *bal-tshuve*, a newly observant Jew who didn't bear the yoke of *yidishkeyt* until long after childhood—you simply can't appreciate the true flavor of a Jewish custom, a Jewish commandment, even if you're docile and good and perform every action with the greatest fervor."

"Oh, go on, Shmuel, you and your nonsense! That's nothing more than what the idlers say behind the oven in the house of study, bleating and philosophizing whether or not anyone is listening. No one's yet proved any of it."

"Prove it? Certainly! I can prove it with piles of examples, with storehouses of facts—tens, hundreds—"

"Good evening! Good evening! What are you so riled up about in here? What's all the fuss? You're apparently so engrossed in your card game that you didn't even hear us come in. This is the second time we've said good evening!"

"Oh, oh, welcome! Welcome, Mister Tudrus, Mister Zerakh, Mister Gimpl, Mister . . . , Mister . . ."

"Hush! On Chanukah no one's a mister. On Chanukah we say Reb Tudrus, Reb Gimpl, just like on Shabbes we say *migdoyl* instead of *magdil*. But that's not the point. The point is, what are you two fellows discussing with so much vigor? Maybe we're interrupting, Reb Shmuel, so don't let us disturb you. If it's something confidential, we'll continue on into the dining room to say good evening to our hostess."

"Not at all! We're not discussing any secrets. Have a seat, fellows, and you'll hear, too. I started telling the story of the miracle that happened to me on Chanukah, that's all."

"Why not? Go ahead, we're listening. But make it quick. After all, it's Chanukah. It's the time to play cards and gamble a little. How does the Bible verse go? 'On all other nights . . . but tonight, everything's gin rummy.' A dollar a minute . . ."

"The story isn't long at all. The whole point isn't even the incident itself but the effect it had on me later. That's why I've developed a habit of mentioning it every year on Chanukah.

"At that time, and maybe today too, for Jewish boys who're stuck in *kheyder* like chickens in cages from early in the morning until nine o'clock at night, there was no better time of year than the eight days of Chanukah. No small thing, Chanukah! You didn't have to study, you got Chanukah *gelt* from your mother and father, from your aunts and uncles, your grandmas and grandpas . . . you played dreidel, you made deals, and if you got really lucky, you also got to halve potatoes and make them into Chanukah lamps for your father—in short, you lived like God in Odessa!

"I remember, it was right then, it was the eighth day, and I was as cheerful as could be. The eight Chanukah lamps that were burning on the windowsill near the door looked to me like the chalices of the golden menorah in the Temple. The wicks shone and sparkled like eight pure stars. Inside the house it was bright and warm; my mother fried chicken fat; the fragrance of cracklings and onions wafted into my nose and tickled it. My father sat with guests around the table, discussing words of Torah. They spoke with their entire bodies, gestured widely, used their thumbs to make a point, got worked up. All in all, it was jovial.

"And what did they talk about? The matter at hand, of course. Every few minutes, a question could be heard above the clamor: 'What's the meaning of Chanukah?' They wrinkled their brows, scrunched up their faces, bit the tips of their beards—but they couldn't answer the question! One of the fellows stood up, quoted something from the Talmud, developed his argument, added new bits of evidence, interpreted it all with enthusiasm, and showed great perspicacity. From all those fine, convoluted speeches, I understood only one thing: The Gentiles polluted all the oil in the Temple, and when the Hasmoneans overpowered them and drove them out, only one small jug of oil sealed with the high priest's seal was left. That jug should have lasted for only one day, but a miracle took place, and the light kept burning for eight full days.

"On account of the fact that I was very drunk that night, and on account of the fact that as far as I was concerned, Chanukah was a grand holiday, I—a pip-squeak, a scamp—lost all fear of my father and of strangers with long beards and cried out like a witness who doesn't even know he's on the stand: 'Big deal! So a jug of oil lasted eight days—that isn't a miracle at all. On the other hand, if one jug had lasted for a whole year, and we could have Chanukah year-round, now that's what I'd call a miracle. We'd be free of our teacher and his slaps and punches . . .'

"Before I had even finished my speech, my father delivered a great, mighty, and terrible smack.

"'You savage! So you want to go wild, run around like a peasant boy, and never do a lick of work? And grow up to be a goy and a boor, eh?' That's what my father shouted, and I would probably have earned a few more good slaps in the face if a miracle hadn't happened: the first slap caused my hat to fly off. Before bending over to try to get hold of it, I naturally had to cover my bare head with the tail of my caftan. Meanwhile, my father's anger flickered out . . . What are you smiling at, Ignatz? Are you making fun of me?"

"On the contrary! I've realized that my earlier complaints were unjustified; that's why I'm smiling now."

"Believe me, dear Ignatz, you're always unjustified whenever you accuse me of that sort of thing. And do you know why? Because, my friend, you're a *bal-tshuve*, and every *bal-tshuve* is a bit of a fanatic, a pest, a fault finder who's beside himself with glee when he catches a flaw in one of his elders, whether it's his father, his grandfather, or some other member of an older generation. No one is as much of an expert in *not* giving the benefit of the doubt as a *bal-tshuve*. And no offense, but it's because *bal-tshuves* don't possess the virtue of patience that they've gotten a bad name and people are leery of getting too close to them."

"Gentlemen, save your quarrel for another time," intervened the guests. "Wrap up the story, and make it quick!"

"Anyway, the slap itself," Shmuel went on, "wouldn't even be worth mentioning if it hadn't ultimately caused an upheaval that led me to discover new ideas. Basically, the slap I received from my father was not in vain. The whole discussion of Chanukah, my father's anger, the unexpected slap—it all remained vivid in my memory and drove me at quite a young age to chew on the question, 'What's the meaning of Chanukah?' Like all little boys, I knew quite well that on Chanukah we recite the prayer *Al hanisim*, and in *Al hanisim* it says, 'In the time of Matisyahu ben Yohanan Hashmonai and his sons the priests, the evil kingdom of the Greeks rose up against the People of Israel to cause them to forget the Holy Torah. And the Blessed Holy One performed a miracle and delivered the strong into the hands of the weak, the evil into the hands of the righteous, and the wanton into the hands of those who study His Torah. Afterward, they purified the sanctuary and kindled lights and instituted the eight-day festival of Chanukah.'

"And here's how I interpreted it: the strong—that's the Greeks—and the weak—that's Matisyahu and his sons and the rest of the faithful Jews: scholars, house-of-study bookworms, like today's *melamdim* for example, or the rabbis and idlers who sit in the house of study and occupy themselves with Torah. The other side naturally went into battle with horses and chariots and we with repentance, prayer, and charity. That there was a Judah Maccabee once upon a time, and that he and his brothers were powerful warriors—that, of course, I had never heard, and my rebbe didn't breathe a word of it either.

"So when I heard the guests debating that night about the meaning of Chanukah, I drew the conclusion that the passage from *Al hanisim* wasn't entirely clear, nor did it answer every question. The story about the single jar of oil that should have lasted only one day but lit the sanctuary for eight didn't make sense either. If that's how it happened, then the miracle itself only lasted for seven days—so why introduce an eight-day holiday?

"And in that way, I puzzled and pondered and searched and sought, until one day I allowed the Evil Impulse to talk me into opening an extracanonical book—a book of Jewish history, in other words. And it was only then that my eyes were opened and I found an answer to my question.

"**AND NOW, MY FRIENDS**, ha-ha, I know what the meaning of Chanukah is!"

1912

EXCERPT FROM **Friendly Fire**

A. B. Yehoshua

As he sets a kettle on the fire, she studies him. The white hair that she remembers from their last meeting has fallen out, and his bald skull, resembling the fashionably shaved heads of young men, arouses in her a slight anxiety.

"I brought you a bunch of newspapers from Israel."

"Newspapers?"

"Also magazines and supplements. The stewardess collected them on the plane and filled a whole bag, so you can pick what interests you."

An ironic smile crosses his face. His eyes flash with a sudden spark.

"Where are they?"

Despite her fatigue, she bends over the suitcase and extracts the bulging bag. For a moment he seems loath to touch it, as if she were handing him a slimy reptile. Then he grabs it and rushes to the boiler, opens a small door revealing tongues of bluish flame, and without delay shoves the entire bag into the fire and quickly shuts the door.

"Wait," she cries, "stop . . ."

"This is where they belong," he smiles darkly at the visitor, with a measure of satisfaction. Her face turns pale. But she keeps her composure, as always.

"Perhaps for you it's where they belong. But before you start burning things, you could warn me."

"Why?"

"Because there was lipstick in there too, which I bought at the airport for my housekeeper."

"Too late," he says quietly, without remorse. "The fire is very hot."

Now she regards him with hostility and resentment. In her parents' house, he was the one who had devoured every old newspaper. But he returns her look with affection.

"Don't be angry. No big deal, just newspapers, which get thrown out anyway. So instead of the trash, I threw them in the fire. You'll compensate your housekeeper with something else. I hope you don't have any more gifts like these in store for me."

"Not a thing," she winces, "that was it. Nothing else. Maybe only . . . candles . . ."

"Candles? Why candles?"

"It's Chanukah now, did you forget? I was thinking, maybe we could light them this week, together . . . It's one of my favorite holidays."

"It's Chanukah? I really didn't know. For some time now I've been cut off from the Jewish calendar. Tonight, for instance, how many candles?"

"It started yesterday, so tonight is the second candle."

"Second candle?" he seems amused that his sister-in-law thought to bring Chanukah candles to Africa. "Where are they? Let's see them."

For a moment she hesitates, but then takes out the box of candles and hands it to him in the odd hope that he might agree to light them here, in the middle of the night, and ease her sudden longing for her husband and children. But again, with the same quick, slightly maniacal movement, he opens the little door and adds the Chanukah candles to the smoldering Israeli newspapers.

"What's the matter with you?" She stands up angrily, but still maintains her calm, as with a student in her class who has done something idiotic.

"Nothing. Don't get angry, Daniela. I've simply decided to take a rest here from all of that."

"A rest from what?"

"From the whole messy stew, Jewish and Israeli . . . Please, don't spoil my rest. After all, you've come to grieve."

"In what way spoil it?" She speaks quietly, without rancor, feeling pity for this big man with the pink bald head.

"You'll find out soon enough what I mean. I want quiet. I don't want to know anything, I want to be disconnected, I don't even want to know the name of the prime minister."

"But you do know."

"I don't, and don't tell me. I don't want to know, just as you don't know the name of the prime minister here in Tanzania, or in China. Spare me all that. Come to think of it, maybe it's too bad I didn't insist that Amotz come with you. I'm afraid you'll get bored here with me on such a long visit."

Now, for the first time, she is offended.

"I won't be bored, don't worry about me. And the visit isn't long, and if it gets hard for you having me here, I'll cut it short and leave earlier. Do what you need to do. I brought a book with me too, and don't you dare throw it in any fire."

"If the book is for you, I won't touch it."

"The nurse you sent to get me warned me . . . By the way, is she really still a pagan?"

"Why still?"

"You mean, she believes in spirits?"

"What's wrong with that?"

"Nothing wrong. A very impressive young woman . . . aristocratic . . ."

"You can't remember, but before the state was established, on street corners in Jerusalem there stood Sudanese like her, very tall and black, wrapped in robes, roasting these wonderful delicious peanuts on little burners, and selling them in cones made of newspaper. But that was before you were born."

"Before I was born . . ."

"Her whole family was murdered in the civil war in southern Sudan, and she grew up to be a woman of great tenderness and humanity."

"Yes. And she said that you didn't come to meet me because you were afraid to run into Israelis. Why would there be Israelis on the plane?"

"On every plane between two points in the world there is at least one Israeli."

"I was the only one on the plane that brought me here."

"Are you sure?"

"I'm sure."

"And a Jew?"

"A Jew?"

"Maybe there was a Jew on the plane?"

"How would I know?"

"Then imagine that I didn't want to run into him either."

"That bad?"

"That bad."

"Why? You're angry at—"

"No, not angry at all, but I am asking for a rest. I'm seventy years old, and I'm allowed to disconnect a bit, and if it's not a final break, then it's a temporary one, or let's call it a time-out. Simply a time out from my people, Jews in general and Israelis in particular."

"And from me too?"

"From you?" He regards his sister-in-law with fondness, pours boiling water into her teacup, puts a flaming match to the cigarette she clenches between her lips, absolutely her last one of the day. "With you I have no choice, you'll always be my Little Sister, as I told you when you were ten. And if you came all the way to Africa to remember Shuli and mourn her with me, it's your right, since I know better than anyone how much you loved her and how much she loved you. That's all. I am warning you, grieve, but do not preach."

2007

Lighting Chanukah Candles in Death's Kingdom

Elie Wiesel

The story we are about to tell has to do with Chanukah. It did not take place during the time of the Hasmoneans and Judah Maccabee, but in our own times.

Additionally, I lived through it myself. Nonetheless, it sounds mysteriously faraway, like a legend from times gone by.

It occurred during the Second World War, in the realm of darkness, somewhere on the ground in Poland's defiled Auschwitz.

December winds were carousing, storming over the camp that looked like a burial ground marked with snow-covered tombstones. The starving, emaciated captives marched out to work knowing that they would be bringing back with them fatalities of frost, illness or just plain weakness.

Older inmates inveighed that it was the cruelest winter of their entire imprisonment. We believed them or we didn't. They probably said the same thing at the beginning of every winter.

But this time reality supported their forecast. People fell like flies during the first piercing phases. The wind froze the blood in their veins, as well as their vision. Death had not yet been as close. It was practically clear that only a selected few would live to see the spring. The majority would succumb. It was simply unbearable. Everything has a limit, including a person's ability to resist.

What was on everyone's mind? To exhaust every possibility of getting a warm shirt for themselves. People sold their crumbs of bread in order to procure some extra *shmattes* to wrap themselves in. Only my bunkmate, the former head of a small Polish town's yeshiva, had other things on his mind.

At first I had no knowledge of it. How could I have known? When I saw his troubled look, his anxiety, I was sure that just like everyone else, he was trying to "organize" an item of clothing, a warmer coat or even a scarf. That's why I didn't even ask him—I had no strength.

In the end, he confided his despair to me: he wasn't managing to find someone to barter with for his portions of bread. So I asked him, what are you looking for? A shirt or a scarf? He looked at me astounded: What are you talking about? God forbid, I'm not a merchant. What was he then looking for? Potatoes and oil. Specifically eight whole potatoes and oil. If it was impossible to get eight, four would do. The four could be cut in half to kindle eight Chanukah lights. I thought he had lost his mind. He had to be crazy to attempt such a thing in the harrowing hell of Auschwitz. But he was strong willed: one mustn't leave a *mitsve* unfulfilled, especially in Auschwitz. Once we neglect observing one, even a small one, there will soon be a second even bigger one. So don't even start.

The teacher in him explained his approach. Doesn't Chanukah symbolize Jewish sacrifice? For the past twenty generations, haven't Jews lit candles to remember the heroism of Judah Maccabee, who was ready to die rather than betray the Torah? Was this really the moment to abandon those teachings? No, no! A thousand times no! It was especially important in our current circumstances to follow their path—to kindle the Jewish people's flames of faith.

In vain I pleaded with him—lighting Chanukah candles was not a mitsve for which you needed to sacrifice your life. But he kept to his response: these times require us to sacrifice ourselves for every mitsve.

Later, quietly, on our pallet, before falling asleep, he said: I'm convinced my point of view is correct. Especially since we don't have any prospects of remaining alive. If I thought that any one of us would survive this enemy, I might have a different opinion. Unfortunately we can't believe in that. So my question is simple:

If we're going to die anyway, why not die for a mitsve, and not just because the murderer wants us to?

Others also tried to talk him out of it. They cited halakhic decisions of all periods, presenting scholarly arguments. But he was well defended and had counterarguments for every challenge. He didn't quite manage to procure either eight nor four whole potatoes. Until . . .

Someone, commiserating, had a conversation with a kitchen worker: Maybe they could help him? Luckily, one of them was *frum*, and brought my bunkmate two raw potatoes with a bit of oil. The potatoes were given to a "specialist" who divided them into the correct portions so that by the next morning, our block was able to light the first Chanukah candle.

The news quickly spread to all the blocks, so naturally people came to make a *brokhe* and marvel at the old-new miracle of persistent Jewish heroism.

The block leader stayed out of it this time, pretending he knew nothing of it. But once he did come to witness my bunkmate's singing of "These Chanukah Lights We Light." Not many participated in the singing—they didn't have the vigor. Only at the lighting of the eighth candle did the entire block take an active part in the ceremony: They were attentive to the brokhe and responded with a zealous *omeyn* and participated with the prayer leader when he chanted popular passages and familiar melodies. That Chanukah wasn't forgotten for a long time. The warmth of the long-extinguished lights remained. If Jews had the fortitude to believe in victory over the Greeks, then we could not now surrender our trust in defeating our enemy. Whether my bunkmate lasted till the end, till liberation—I do not know. I lost sight of him during the January evacuation.

But I did not forget his act of courage. Year in, year out, when the world is celebrating Chanukah, I remember him.

And that is why I am now telling you this story. But let me quickly correct an error: The story did occur in Judah Maccabee's time. And I am a witness of it.

1969

Chanukah Money

Sholom Aleichem

-ONE-

GUESS, CHILDREN, WHICH HOLIDAY is the best holiday of all?

Chanukah, of course!

Eight days in a row with no school, eating latkes with goose fat, playing at dreidel, and receiving Chanukah money from everyone—so, I ask you, could there be a better holiday?

Winter. Outdoors, it is cold; the frost burns fiercely; the windows are frozen over, decorated with beautiful frost trees; and inside, the house is cozy and warm. The silver Chanukah menorah has stood ready since early morning. Father paces from room to room, his hands clasped behind him as he recites the evening prayers. After standing still for the Eighteen Benedictions, he removes from a table drawer a wax candle, the *shamash*, to light the others with, and as he recites the concluding prayer, he signals to me and my younger brother, Mottel, for he is forbidden to speak until the prayer is over.

"Ee-aw! *Shehu noteh shamayim vayosed Haaretz*—He stretched forth the heavens and laid the foundations of the earth—Ee-nu-aw!"

Mottel and I do not understand what he means, and we ask:

"What do you want? A match?"

Father points toward the kitchen.

"Ee-aw-aw! *V'al keyn n'kaveh l'kho*—We therefore hope in Thee—Ee-aw-nu!"

"What? A bread knife? A pair of scissors?"

"Mm-ay-ee-aw-nu-feh! *Bayom hahu yihyeh adonoy ekhud u'shmo ekhod*—On that day the Lord shall be One, and His name One . . . Your mother! Call your mother, let her hear the blessing over the Chanukah candles."

My brother I tear out of the room, almost falling over each other.

"Mama! Hurry, Chanukah candles!"

"Oy, God help me, Chanukah candles!" exclaims my mother, abandoning all her work in the kitchen (dressing geese, rendering goose fat, frying latkes), and hurries out into the parlor. And right behind her is Brayne, the scullery maid, a swarthy woman with a mustache, a full face, and forever-greasy hands. Mother stands off to the side and takes on a pious expression while Brayne remains standing at the door, wiping her greasy hands on her soiled apron and smearing her nose with her greasy hand, thus leaving a black smudge across her whole face. We have to be stronger than iron, I and my brother, Mottel, to hold ourselves in and not burst out laughing.

Father holds the lit shamash candle near the Chanukah menorah, leans over, and chants the blessing in the familiar tune: "*Boruch atoh!*—Blessed art Thou!" and finishes with, "*l'hadlik nair shel Chanukah!*—to kindle the Chanukah candles."

Mother responds with awe in her voice, "*Borukh hu u'borukh sh'mo, amen*—Blessed be He and blessed be His name, amen," and Brayne nods her head in approval, all the while making such odd faces that my brother, Mottel, and I are afraid to look at each other.

"*Haneyros haleylo sh'onu madlikin*—the candles that we kindle tonight," Father sings under his breath as he paces back and forth around the room, glancing at the Chanukah menorah and praying and praying on and on at great length. We are hoping for it to end soon so he will put his hand in his pocket and take out his purse. We exchange winks and nudge each other.

"Mottel, you go over and ask him for Chanukah money."

"How come *I* have to ask for Chanukah money?"

"Because you're younger, so *you* have to ask for Chanukah money."

"Maybe it's the other way around. You're older, so *you* have to ask for Chanukah money."

Father knows all too well that we are whispering about Chanukah money, but he pretends not to hear. Calmly, unhurriedly, he goes over to the table drawer and begins counting money. A little shiver passes over our bodies, our hands tremble, our hearts pound. We look up at the ceiling, scratch behind our sidelocks, and try to look indifferent, as if this has nothing to do with us.

Father gives a little cough. "Hm . . . children, come over here."

"What? What's the matter?"

"Here's your Chanukah money."

Now that we have our Chanukah money, off we run, I and Mottel, at first slowly, composed and well mannered, but then faster and faster, with a hop and a skip and a jump. By the time we reach our room we can barely control ourselves. We do three handsprings each and hop on one foot as we chant:

Eynge, beynge
Stupe, tzeynge,
Gole shvartze,
Eymeli, reymeli,
Beygeli, feygeli—
Hup!

OUT OF GREAT JOY and elation, we slap ourselves twice on the cheeks.

The door opens and in comes Uncle Benny.

"Hey, you scamps, I owe you Chanukah money!"

Uncle Benny puts his hand in his vest pocket, takes out two silver gulden, and gives us our Chanukah money.

-TWO-

NO ONE ON EARTH would ever think that Father and Uncle Benny were brothers. Father is tall and thin, while Uncle Benny is short and chubby; Father is dark, Uncle Benny fair; Father is somber and untalkative, Uncle Benny jolly and a chatterer. They are as different as night and day, summer and winter, yet they are brothers.

Father gets a large sheet of paper, rules off black and white squares, and asks for black and white beans from the kitchen. This will serve as a checker game.

Mother is in the kitchen rendering goose fat and frying latkes. I and my brother, Mottel, are playing at dreidel, spinning the dreidel to see which word— *Nes Godol Haya Shom*—will appear when it stops spinning, and Father and Uncle Benny sit down to play checkers.

"There's just one thing I must insist on, Benny: No changing your mind, do you hear! Once you make a move, it's final!" says Father.

"A move is a move," says Uncle Benny, and makes a move.

"A move is a move," agrees Father, and takes one of Benny's checkers.

"A move is a move," says Uncle Benny, and takes two of Father's checkers.

The longer the game goes on, the more deeply engrossed in the game they become, chewing on their beards, jiggling their legs under the table, and both humming the same tune as they consider their next moves.

"Oy, what to do, what to do, what to do?" chants Father with a tune from the Gemorah while gnawing at the tip of his beard. "If I move here, he'll move there. If I move there, he'll move here. So I had better make this move!"

"What a move, what a move!" Uncle Benny helps him out in the same tune.

"Why should I be afraid!" Father sings on. "If he takes my checker, I'll take two of his. Aha! But what if he has in mind to take three of my checkers?"

"Three checkers, three checkers, three checkers?" Uncle Benny joins in.

"Oy, you're a fool, Benny, a fool and a great one!" sings Father, and makes a move.

"You're a fool yourself, brother, and an even greater one!" sings Uncle Benny, making a move and immediately grabbing his checker back.

"*Feh*, Benny, I thought we decided, a move is a move!" says Father, now without a tune, and grabs Uncle Benny's hand.

"That didn't count," protests Uncle Benny. "So long as I'm still making a move, I can go wherever I please!"

"No," exclaims Father. "A move is final! We did decide that, Benny. No changing your mind, Benny!"

"No changing your mind?" says Uncle Benny. "How many times do you change your mind?"

"I?" says Father. "Eh, Benny, that's why I hate to play checkers with you!"

"So who is forcing you to play with me?"

"Already? You're fighting over a little bean again?" Mother cries, and comes in from the kitchen, her face aflame, and in her footsteps, Brayne, bearing a large platter of steaming latkes drenched in goose fat. We all head for the table. I and my brother, Mottel, who just before had been scrapping like cat and dog, quickly make peace and sit down to eat the latkes with great gusto.

-THREE-

AT NIGHT I LIE on my bed and think: How much would it add up to if, let us say, all the uncles and all the aunts and all the other relatives were to give me Chanukah money? First of all there is Uncle Moshe-Aaron, Mother's brother, a tightfisted but rich man. Then there's Uncle Itzi and Aunt Dvorya, with whom Father and Mother have been angry for years and years. And what about Uncle Beynish and Aunt Yente! And let's not forget our sister, Eydel. And her husband, Sholem-Zeydel. And all the other relations.

"Mottel, are you sleeping!"

"Yes. What is it?"

"How much do you think Uncle Moshe-Aaron will give us for Chanukah money?"

"How would I know? Am I a prophet?"

A minute later: "Mottel, are you sleeping?"

"Yes. What is it?"

"Does anyone in the world have as many uncles and aunts as we do?"

"Maybe yes, maybe no."

Two minutes later: "Mottel, are you sleeping?"

"Yes. What is it?"

"If you're sleeping, how can you talk to me?"

"You're asking me questions, so I have to answer you."

Three minutes later: "Mottel, are you sleeping?"

"*Tss-trrr-khilkhilkhil-tsss* . . ."

Mottel is snoring, gurgling, whistling through his nose, and I sit up in my bed, take out my money, smooth it out, and examine it.

Just think, I say to myself, it's only a piece of paper, yet what can't you buy with it: toys, penknives, little canes, purses, nuts and sweets, raisins and carob—whatever you want.

I hide my money under my pillow and say my night prayers, and Brayne comes in from the kitchen bearing a full platter of money. Brayne is not walking, but floating on air, chanting, "*hanayros halaylo sh'onu madlikin . . .*" and Mottel is swallowing rubles as if they were stuffed cabbages. "Mottel!" I yell with all my might, "God help you, Mottel, what are you doing? *Rubles?*"

I wake up and spit three times to ward off evil. "*Tfoo-tfoo-tfoo*—a dream!*"

And I fall back to sleep.

-FOUR-

THE FOLLOWING MORNING after prayers and breakfast, Mother dresses us in our little fur-lined jackets and bundles us up in large, warm shawls, and we are on our way to collect Chanukah money, first, as always, from Uncle Moshe-Aaron.

Uncle Moshe-Aaron is not a well man. He is always suffering from indigestion; whenever you come, you always find him at the washstand, wiping his hands and muttering a prayer, *Asher yotzer.*

"Good morning, Uncle Moshe-Aaron!" we both cry out together, I and my brother, Mottel, as we are met by Aunt Pessl, a tiny woman with one black eye and the other white. I should say, one eyebrow black, the other white. Aunt Pessl removes our jackets and unwinds us from our shawls and blows our noses in her apron.

"Blow!" says Aunt Pessl. "Good, good blow! Don't hold back! More! More! That's the way!"

Uncle Moshe-Aaron, wearing a quilted yarmulke on his head and an old fur frock coat, with cotton stuffed in his ears and with a sparse mustache, is at the washstand drying his hands, grimacing, blinking his eyes, and straining as he says his prayers.

I and Mottel sit down in agony. We always have feelings of dread and chills whenever we come here. Aunt Pessl sits opposite us, clasps her hands over her heart, and starts to grill us.

"How is your father?"

"Fine."

"How is your mother?"

"Fine."

"Did she dress the geese?"

"Dressed."

"Rendered goose fat?"

"Rendered."

"Fried latkes?"

"Fried."

"Uncle Benny visited?"

"Visited."

"Played checkers?"

"Played."

And so on.

Aunt Pessl blows our noses again and says to Uncle Moshe-Aaron, "Moshe-Aaron, you need to give them some Chanukah money."

Uncle Moshe-Aaron doesn't hear; he is still drying his hands, straining to finish his prayers.

Aunt Pessl isn't loath to remind him again. "Moshe-Aaron, Chanukah money for the children!"

"Hah, what?" Uncle Moshe-Aaron sputters, moving the cotton from one ear to the other.

"Chanukah money for the children!" Aunt Pessl shouts right into his ear.

"Oy, my sto-omach! My sto-omach!" Uncle Moshe-Aaron draws out the word painfully and grabs his stomach with both hands. "It's Chanukah money you want? Why do children need money? What will you do with money? Hah? Squander it, throw it away, hah? How much Chanukah money did your father give you? Hah?"

"A ruble for me," I say, "and half a ruble for him."

"A ruble? Hm . . . they spoil kids rotten, they ruin them! What will you do with the ruble? Hah? Spend it? Hah? Don't spend it! Do you hear what I'm telling you? Don't spend it! Maybe you want to spend it, hah?"

"Spend it or not spend it, what difference does it make to you?" Aunt Pessl breaks in. "Give them what they're supposed to get, and let them go in peace."

Uncle Moshe-Aaron goes off to his room, shuffling in his slippers, searches through all the drawers and cupboards, and scrapes out a few small coins, muttering to himself:

"Hm . . . they spoil children rotten, they ruin them, utterly ruin them!"

He shoves a few old coins into our palms. Aunt Pessl puts on our jackets, wraps us in the large, warm shawls, and we are on our way.

We dash across the white, frozen, crackly snow and try to count the old coins that Uncle Moshe-Aaron has shoved into our hands, but we cannot manage it. Our hands are frozen, red, stiff. The coins are large, heavy, copper coins, the six-ers from olden times, the three-ers worn thin, the groschens old-fashioned, thick, and moldy. It is difficult, impossible, to figure out in the frost how much Chanukah money Uncle Moshe-Aaron has given us!

-FIVE-

OUR SECOND STOP for collecting Chanukah money is at Uncle Itzi and Aunt Dvoyra, the ones Mother and Father have been angry with for years and years. Why they are angry, we do not know. We only know that Father and Uncle Itzi (blood brothers) never speak to each other, even though they both pray at the same synagogue and both sit right next to each other on the same bench, cheek by jowl. When a holiday comes and the Torahs are taken from the Ark and the auctioning begins for selling the *aliyas*, the special honors for blessing the Torah, they always try to outbid each other, both wanting to recite the very same blessing. At the time the synagogue is filled with the excitement of a carnival, everyone is talking, nudging one another, whispering, laughing, and egging on the bidders. Everyone is eager to find out which one will win *shishi*, the sixth blessing before the reading of the Torah, or the *moftir*, the reading of the lesson from the Prophets. When the bidding begins to heat up, the congregation urges them to bid to the limit. The sexton, Mekhtshi Funfatch, with the red elflocks, stands on the dais bent over, his prayer shawl constantly slipping down his shoulders, his yarmulke awry; he glances toward the eastern wall, where Father and Uncle Itzi are seated, and he chants in his nasal voice, "Eighteen gulden for the sixth honor! Twenty gulden for the sixth honor! Twenty-two gulden for the sixth honor!"

Father and Uncle Itzi sit, one facing this way, one facing that, both pretending to be absorbed in their texts, but whatever one bids, the other tops. The congregation is enjoying every minute of this rivalry and joins in gleefully, "Thirty, thirty! Thirty-five! Thirty-seven! Forty, forty!"

Mekhtshi Funfatch looks from one to the other. "Forty gulden for the sixth honor! Forty-five gulden for the sixth honor!"

Father and Uncle Itzi continue to outbid each other. They are already up to fifty gulden. Mekhtshi raises his hand and is about to conclude the bidding in favor of Father, "Fifty guld—en!"

But Uncle Itzi reconsiders and raises a finger, the congregation all helping out: "Fifty-one! Fifty-one!" And on it goes, until at long last, the bidding has reached some sixty gulden (no one has ever heard of such an amount!) and the sixth honor belongs to Uncle Itzi. When it is time to auction off the moftir, Father looks at the shamash and signals with his hand to indicate that the moftir is *his*! For Mekhtshi this is fine, but you can be sure that the congregation isn't in agreement. You have to bid, that's the way it is. That's why it's a holiday. There's no monopoly, no automatic claim on the moftir!

"Ten gulden for the moftir! Fifteeen gulden for the moftir! Twenty gulden for the moftir! Fifty gulden for the moftir!"

Quite a jump! Father turns his head. Who is this intruding into his moftir? You can guess it is again Uncle Itzi vying with Father; he wants to buy the moftir for his young son-in-law. Oh no you don't! You can't have both the shishi and the moftir! Two honors is one too many! Father stands, and winks to the shamash.

"A hundred!"

The word *hundred* flies through the synagogue like thunder and lightning. The entire congregation is stunned, amazed. Such a high bid for a moftir has not been offered since the synagogue has been in existence.

And Mekhtshi forges on with his job. "A hundred gulden for moftir! A hundred gulden for moftir! A hundred gulden . . ." (He is eager to close the bidding.)

Uncle Itzi stands up. Father gives him a strange look, as if saying, Are you crazy or out of your mind? Is it a fight you want? Then let's fight!

Uncle Itzi sits down, and the moftir remains ours . . .

Still and all, when there is family celebration at our house or at Uncle Itzi's—a birth, a bar mitzvah, a *bris*, a *pidyn haben*, an engagement party, a calling up to the Torah on the day of a wedding, a marriage or a divorce—they go to each other's homes; each has a seat of honor, they exchange gifts, wish one another well, and dance together with all the family in a circle.

"A good morning to you, Uncle Itzi! A good morning to you, Aunt Dvoyra!" we exclaim together, I and my brother, Mottel, and we are taken up as very welcome guests.

"I'm sure you two aren't here to recite the Haggadah, but for something else . . ." Uncle Itzi says to us. He pinches our cheeks, takes out a little change purse, and gives us Chanukah money, for me a bright silver twenty-kopek piece, and for Mottel, a bright silver twenty-kopek piece, and we are on our way to Uncle Beynish's house.

-SIX-

IF YOU CAN IMAGINE a true hell, that is Uncle Beynish's house. No matter when you arrive, you will find complete bedlam, utter chaos, earsplitting noise. There is a house full of children: half-naked, filthy, hair unwashed, bruised, scratched-up, sickly children with dark circles under their eyes. This one is laughing and that one is crying, this one is singing and that one is shrieking, this one is whooping and that one is whistling, this one is wearing his father's coat with its sleeves rolled up and that one is riding on a broomstick, this one is drinking milk from a pitcher and that one is cracking nuts, this one is walking around with a herring head and that one is sucking a candy as two rivulets flow from his nose into his mouth. Aunt Yente has to be stronger than iron to be able to endure this crew. She curses them, she pinches them, she grabs them hard. She isn't picky: Whoever is close at hand is the one who receives the slap, the shove, the pick in the side.

A slap is commonplace. "Choke! The devil take you!" are minor curses; it is not unusual to hear words like *plague, cholera,* and *convulsions* and yet somehow they are spoken with good humor, in the same tone as if she was saying, "Good Shabbes."

The only time it gets quiet is when Uncle Beynish comes home. But as Uncle Beynish is a very busy man, tending his shop all day and coming home only for a quick bite to eat, the house is always in an uproar.

As we arrive, we find Ezriel'ke (the middle one) riding astride Getzi (the eldest), with Froyke and Mendel (two younger ones) whipping them on, one with the sleeve of a cotton shirt, the other with the cover of some prayer book. Chaym'l (a middle child between Froyke and Mendel) has found the windpipe of a slaughtered goose, has inflated it with his last breath until he is almost blue in the face, and has managed to produce a weird squeal from it like that of a stuck pig. Zeinvil'le (I don't know whether he is an older or a younger child) is playing a concert on a comb, and Duvid'l (a little four-year-old), wearing his boots on his hands, is beating time on the floor with them. Sender'l is carrying a kitten by the scruff of the neck, its little tongue sticking out, its eyes shut, its legs outstretched, as if saying: Look what they do to me! They torture me, torture me!

Esther'l (the oldest girl) wants to comb Khaski's (the younger girl's) hair, to make a braid, but as Khaski's hair is very thick and curly and has gone long uncombed, she refuses, and is crying lustily as she receives slap after slap from her sister. The only quiet one is Pinny'le, a tiny lad with bowed legs, with the shirttail out of his trousers. The problem with him is that he's been there. But none of this bothers Aunt Yente. She sits calmly at the table with two infants, one nursing, the other sitting on her lap, as she sips her chicory.

"May God bless your little bones!" she croons fondly to the suckling baby, and clasps it lovingly to her breast while shoving the elder one on her lap roughly. "Look at the way you're eating—may the worms eat you! Esther'l, Rakh'tzi, Khaski, where are you when I need you? Quick, wipe his nose; wash a saucer out for me, I'm drinking without a saucer! Give him a smack for me that he'll really feel! Dear heart of mine, my soul, my joy! Their mouths never shut! All morning long all they do is eat, may the devil take them!"

When they see me and Mottel, the children fall on us like locusts, some grabbing our hands, some our legs, some our heads. Chaym'l lets the air out of the inflated goose windpipe right into my ear, and Duvid'l grabs me around the waist with both boots. Tiny Pinny'le with the shirttail out of his trousers latches on to one of my legs, winding himself around it like a snake, and a pandemonium of shouts envelops us in a loud din.

"May your teeth hurt from screaming!" cries Aunt Yente from the other room. "A person can go deaf around here! They're devils, not children, may their souls burn!"

Aunt Yente screams and the children scream—everyone screams. Suddenly Uncle Beynish arrives with his tallis and tefillin—his prayer shawl and phylacteries—apparently coming from the prayer house. In a split second there is absolute silence, and the entire gang vanishes from sight.

"A good morning to you, Uncle Beynish!" we exclaim, I and my brother, Mottel.

"What are you scamps doing here? I'll bet you're after some Chanukah money!" Uncle Beynish says, taking out his purse and handing us a silver ten-kopek coin.

The children peek out from the corners of the room like cockroaches, stare at us like little mice, wink at us and signal with their fingers while making funny faces to get us to laugh. We barely contain ourselves, and flee from this hell.

We continue on our way for Chanukah money to our sister, Eydel.

Our sister, Eydel, and her husband, Sholem-Zeydel, may they rest in peace, are long in the Next World.

Since early childhood, Eydel was always a weepy soul; over the least little nothing she would cry her heart out, shedding copious tears for her own as well as for others' woes. But once she became engaged to Sholem-Zeydel, she never ceased crying. Perhaps you think it was because she wasn't pleased with her bridegroom? God forbid! Did she know him enough not to be pleased with him? It was simply assumed a bride must cry before the wedding. When the tailors brought the wedding dress to be fitted, she wept all night. Later on, at the engagement party given by her girlfriends—when they began the dancing, she kept running off to her room to bury her head in her pillow for a good cry. Don't even *ask* about what happened on the day of the wedding! That was *her* day. She never stopped crying. But the supreme moment came at the veiling ceremony, when Menasha Fiddele, the *klezmer*, seated her on the bridal chair and Reb Boruch, the *bodkhin*, the traditional entertainer of brides who prepares them for the reality of married life, mounted the table, folded his hands across his stomach, lowered his head as one does when grieving the dead, and sang a beautiful mournful tune that would have moved a stone to tears:

Dear bride! Lovely bride!
Let your tears flow,

Let them stream from your eyes,
Let your sad beauty show.
Soon you will stand beneath the canopy,
Your head bowed low
In innocence before the wedding vows.
But after, you will too soon know
What the rest have known for a long, long time:
Our lives are full of bitterness
Here below.
A human being is not made of stone
But of ache and woe,
Of flesh and blood,
Through and through.
The wicked suffer whippings in hell,
Blow upon blow,
Their weeping and wailing and crying out
Grow and grow.
You must yourself be virtuous,
Hold yourself low.
Let your tears be humble,
Let your sad eyes flow.

And in this mode he went on and on.

All the women, both relatives and friends, who stood hovering over her, helping unloosen the bride's lovely thick hair, made ridiculous faces, pursed their lips, blew their noses, and wiped their eyes while poor Eydel wailed and sobbed, carrying on so that she fainted three times and was barely revived with great effort.

But as weepy as our sister was, our brother-in-law, Sholem-Zeydel, was cheerful, lively, a practical joker, a wag, and, may he forgive me, a pain in the neck. He loved to tease, to flick other people's noses or ears—he thought that was the greatest fun. How many times did we, I and my brother, Mottel, go around with throbbing ears. We were thrilled to death when we heard that the two of them would no longer be supported by my father in our house and would be moving to their own place. The day they moved, our house was in a state of utter chaos. Eydel was in tears, bemoaning her fate, while Mother joined her. And Sholem-Zeydel, who was going through the motions of packing their belongings, kept leaping about, slyly stealing up on us for a flick to the tip of the nose or to the back of the ear. He finally left, and had the audacity to tell us not to wait long for an invitation but to be frequent visitors! We promised ourselves never to set eyes on him again!

But people forget everything, especially a flick on the nose. How could we not go for Chanukah money to our own brother-in-law?

When we arrive at Eydel's, Sholem-Zeydel greets us with a broad "Look who's here! What's the good word? You did the right thing to come here. I've got some Chanukah money for you!"

And Sholem-Zeydel removes from his change purse some coins and places a few newly minted, shiny silver coins right into our palms, and before we even have a chance to count them out, we have received several flicks, first I to the tip of the nose and then Mottel to the back of the ear, then Mottel to the tip of the nose and I to the back of the ear.

"Stop tormenting these poor children!" our sister, Eydel, pleads with tears in her eyes. She draws us off to the side and fills our pockets with honey cake, nuts, and carob and throws in some extra Chanukah money.

We take to our heels and race home.

-SEVEN-

SO, MOTTEL, LET'S get to work and figure out how much Chanukah money we have. But do you know what? You be quiet; first I'll count out my share, and then you count yours."

And I count: "A ruble and three twenty-kopek pieces, and four zlotys, and five grivnis, and six pitakes. How much does that make? Looks like it's a ruble and three twenty-kopek pieces, four zlotys, five grivnis, and six pitakes . . ."

My brother, Mottel, can't wait till I add mine all up, and he begins adding up *his* haul; he transfers the coins from one hand to the other, counting, "A twenty-kopek piece and a twenty-kopek piece comes to two twenty-kopek pieces, plus another twenty-kopek piece adds up to three twenty-kopek pieces, plus two gulden are three twenty-kopek pieces and two gulden, and a grivni plus another grivni and another grivni—comes to two twenty-kopek pieces, three gulden, I mean three gulden and two twenty-kopek pieces. Tphoo! What am I talking about? I have to start all over again from the beginning!"

And he begins from the beginning. We add and add and it doesn't add up. We count and count and it doesn't come out right. When we get to Uncle Moshe-Aaron's old pitakes, heavy six-kopek coins, rubbed-out three-kopek coins, and fat groschens, we get so mixed up in our counting that we have no way of figuring out what we have. We try to exchange these old coins with Mother, with Father, with Brayne, the cook—it won't work! No one wants to touch them!

"What kind of pitakes are these? Who gave you these old coins?"

We are ashamed to tell who, and remain silent. "Do you know what I think we should do?" Mottel says to me. "Let's take them into the oven or throw them in the snow so no one will find them."

"Pretty clever!" I say to him. "Wouldn't it be smarter to give them to some beggar?"

But just our luck—no beggar is in sight! What has become of all the beggars who claw at your coattails, who plead with you for another kopek, who curse and harangue? No, once you need something, it will never happen! Never! Never!

1899

Chanukah, Why?

Emma Green

As far as holidays go, Chanukah is a disaster. Contrary to the popular public-school-kid myth, eight days of presents doesn't mean the holiday is super-Christmas; it means the presents are junk, a proliferation of trash. Dreidl is a terrible game that requires no strategy and practically no skill. Somehow, the world's entire gelt supply seems to have been manufactured in 1993, so even if you *do* win, your reward is stale, filmy-white, subpar chocolate. Worst of all, Jews are forever manufacturing kitschy alternatives to Christmas customs: What's with the Chanukah bear, anyways? Arguably, latkes are one merit of the Festival of Lights, but woe to the holiday that relies upon potatoes as its only defense.

The story of Chanukah doesn't even appear in the Torah—the books of 1 and 2 Maccabees are in the Catholic Bible, not the Hebrew one. The saga is briefly described in the Talmud—a tale of armed Jewish rebellion against the Hellenistic King Antiochus IV, paired with a parable about miracle oil that kept the eternal flame of the Temple burning for eight nights when it should have lasted only for one. It is both theologically thin and celebratory of violent nationalism. For most of Jewish history, the holiday has been of little consequence. "Chanukah is . . . a minor holiday that America has elevated into something much more," said Joshua Plaut, the head rabbi at the Reform Metropolitan

Synagogue in New York City. "Jews have been part of that magnification of Chanukah. It suits our purposes."

So why, in America, has Chanukah taken on outsized significance? Because it serves a particular purpose: an opportunity to negotiate the twin, competing pressures of ethnic tension and assimilation. As the Rowan University historian Dianne Ashton writes in her book, *Hanukkah in America*, "Hanukkah's strongest American advocates seem to have been those who felt the complexities of American Jewish life most acutely." It's so simple, so conveniently vague, that it has been used by rabbis, advertisers, Zionists, Hebrew school teachers, and parents to promote everything from ethnic pride and nationalism to engagement in Jewish life and buying stuff.

No doubt, Chanukah is an incredibly important part of the story of Jews in America. Why, then, is this holiday—the most public Jewish celebration in the United States—so silly?

LIKE MUCH OF JEWISH AMERICAN life, Chanukah's evolution in the United States is a story of immigrants. In the nineteenth century, the Jewish population in the United States was very small—roughly 250,000 by 1880, Ashton estimates. As different groups of immigrant Jews came to the country from central and Eastern Europe, a debate emerged: "What is going to be the form of Judaism that will thrive in the United States?" Ashton said. Many of the institutions of Jewish life, such as schools and synagogues, were in Europe; coming to America was starting over, and in a very new context. "Freedom of religion was a shocking experience," she said. "Jews had not encountered that before."

In the middle of the nineteenth century, some of the first Jews to promote Chanukah in America were the rabbis who led the Reform Movement, which was largely based in Cincinnati, Ohio. Their Judaism was intellectual and sermon-heavy—"it really had nothing for the kids," Ashton said. So "they came up with this idea of a synagogue festival for kids at Hanukkah as a way to interest kids in the synagogue: candle-lighting, singing songs, teaching the kids little skits, and then treating them to oranges and ice cream."

During this period in American history, Chanukah wasn't really celebrated in the home beyond the lighting of the menorah, Ashton said, but it did have certain domestic qualities. "The rabbis would stand up in the front [of the synagogue] and talk to the kids, but the women organized the kids, and fed the kids, and taught the kids the songs," she said. This, in itself, was another way of reinforcing synagogue life, creating a role for women in promoting children's education.

This was in keeping with a larger trend in American culture: a sentimental Victorian fascination with domesticity. A number of home-based festivals, such as birthday parties, emerged in the second half of the nineteenth century, and Chanukah crept toward the home along similar lines. One of the Cincinnati rabbis, Isaac Mayer Wise, purposefully played into this. Over the course of thirty-nine weeks around 1860, he serialized a romance novel based on the story of the Maccabees, playing into Victorian tropes like "religious virtues, patriotism, and strong gender distinctions," Ashton writes. This was a way of educating Jews about Chanukah, but it was also a form of reassurance: Yes, Jews could be part of American culture.

Elsewhere in the United States, some Jewish communities were wary of their surrounding culture. "Immigrant Jews had a deep and abiding anxiety about Christmas—this commercialized, merry, fun, sparkly Christmas was altogether new to them," said Jenna Weissman Joselit, a professor of history at George Washington University. Toward the end of the nineteenth century, as more and more kids entered public schools, this fear grew. "The Yiddish press, particularly the *Jewish Daily Forward*, sought to explain America to these new immigrants," she said. "They spent a lot of time trying to defang Christmas and assuage any concerns that a pogrom was at their doorstep." Memories lingered from events like the Warsaw pogrom of 1881 when Jewish businesses were destroyed and their owners attacked for two days around Christmas time.

If only by an accident of timing, Chanukah served as a counterbalance to this fear of Christmas in Jewish communities—its celebration was a way of asserting Jewish identity. There may have been mild elements of competition to it, too. "That's the cheap and dirty way of looking at it—that Chanukah is penis envy, that Jews need to have their own equivalent of Christmas," Weissman Joselit said. But it also marked all sorts of other things, such as Jews' economic success, especially in places like New York City. "Immigrants needed reassurance that they were succeeding, that this gamble of coming to the U.S., to this new country an ocean away from everyone they know, was worth [it]," Ashton said. "One measure of success was being able to buy presents for their children."

And so the Chanukah industry emerged. Yiddish newspapers made money by running advertisements for gifts—"'presents' was one of the earliest words that appeared in English in Yiddish newspapers," Ashton said. Restaurant owners crafted special dishes for the holiday; shopkeepers made toys for parents to buy. This commercialization had the effect of "undermining traditional religious authority, empowering ordinary Jews, and tying religion inextricably to the market," Ashton wrote.

As Jews suburbanized in the middle of the century, the holiday suburbanized along with them, Weissman Joselit said. The kid-centered-ness of Chanukah fit well with broader *Leave It To Beaver* norms of American culture. "I came across recipes [from] the '40s and '50s: little Maccabees fashioned out of cottage cheese or tuna fish," she said.

As Chanukah grew, so did the complexities of American Judaism. The holiday had been connected with Zionism for decades before the 1950s; Theodor Herzl, one of the founders of the movement, "placed the celebration of Hanukkah in the center of the modern Jew's capacity to bolster one's own self-respect while living as a minority," Ashton writes. But particularly in the '60s and '70s, American Jews found urgency in the story of the Maccabees because of political affairs in Israel, Weissman Joselit said. Once again, some believed, Jews were an embattled minority in a strange land. Once again, their fate was unsure.

Too, many Jews felt like an embattled minority in the United States. "There was a commitment in American Jewry writ large, based on the European experience, that a mixture of government and religion just never augured well for the Jews," said Marc Stern, a lawyer at the American Jewish Committee. "That mix was ideologically repugnant."

"The religious events that have more significance—you can't play around with them as easily."

In the 1970s and '80s, these feelings contributed to a curious set of legal battles within the Jewish community. In 1973, the Chabad-Lubavitch Rebbe Menachem M. Schneerson began a campaign: Help Jews across America light the menorah on Chanukah. Religious law commands Jews to light the menorah on Chanukah, preferably in public. In addition to distributing tin candleholders, the organization orchestrated and sponsored menorah lightings in American parks, city halls, and village greens—on government-held land, in other words. By 1979, President Jimmy Carter was participating in a lighting ceremony.

These public displays made many Jews uncomfortable. The Chabad campaign tested the "bulk of the Jewish community's repudiation of the separation of church and state," Stern said. "As a tactic, it was thought that the best way to avoid Christian symbols—with all their power, because they're the majority, they're the norm, and because in many places we weren't going to match them one-for-one—[was] if we simply gave up on government and did our own thing." And always, there was that lingering fear of violence against the Jewish community. "There were still, twenty-five, thirty years ago, Jews who believed: Keep your head down. Don't call attention to yourself. The menorah campaign was a challenge to that attitude," he said.

Working at the time with the American Jewish Congress, Stern was part of the team of litigators who submitted court briefs in opposition to Chabad's menorahs, including the 1989 Supreme Court case *County of Allegheny v. ACLU*. The case was a little bizarre. The court considered two displays, one crèche and one eighteen-foot menorah. Five years earlier, it had ruled in the case *Lynch v. Donnelly* that nativity scenes and other religious displays on government property were generally okay. In *Allegheny*, "the court somehow ended up with the weirdest of all possible results," Stern said, "which was that the menorah was okay, and this crèche was not." The justices reasoned while the nativity scene displayed language designed primarily to promote religion, the menorah did not.

In other words: Chabad won. Today, these giant menorahs are just a part of the American winter landscape. The White House menorah lighting is an annual tradition. No doubt, this public visibility has been one reason why Chanukah has risen in prominence in American culture. But there's also an irony here. Chabad exists to help Jews engage with Jewish life, yet the holiday that Chabad most visibly promotes—Chanukah—is one of the least liturgically important holidays of the year. "Chabad can't be doing things at the White House on Yom Kippur because they're in shul," Ashton said. "The religious events that have more significance and that are under more control by the clergy—you can't play around with [them] as easily."

As far as the options for Jewish gateway holidays go, Chanukah is a pretty poor choice. Some, like Chabad, explicitly intend for it to be a means of drawing Jews into observance, yet there's not much theological or ritual complexity to the celebration. For many Jews, it's a fraught time of year, full of identity contests that match plastic yard reindeers against giant light-up menorahs; as Ashton put it, "There's a lot about display in December." This public performance gives the holiday a distinct air of *trying too hard*: to compete with Christmas, to be colorful and loud, to demonstrate Jewishness, all without having to deal with Jewish theology, law, or morals. It has become a blue-and-white kaleidoscope of vague Jewishness, one that tacitly enables Christmas-style material excess.

ANY EXAMINATION OF CHANUKAH'S ROLE in American Jewish life is inevitably self-parody. What more Jewish question could there be than *Is this good for the Jews?* But Judaism is a forward-looking religion; all its great dilemmas take place on an infinite Mount Nebo, one generation looking to the Promised Land and wondering what will become of the next.

It's a little much to claim that Chanukah hinders the continuation of the Jewish people. But this is a holiday that is all about children and their education, especially in America. For some Jews, Chanukah is the only time of year when they engage with their heritage. Plaut, the congregational rabbi in New York who also wrote the book *A Kosher Christmas*, spent many years as a campus rabbi at the Hillels of MIT and Trinity College in Connecticut. In his experience, Chanukah celebrations "usually brought in nonreligious students on campus to celebrate Chanukah. That probably comes from what they experienced as children, growing up," he said. Where there's an event that might involve drinking and food, there are young people, and for rabbis, this presents a rare opportunity. "In the world we live in, you take people when they come to you, and you try and create the need for them constantly. Chanukah is an easy, non-threatening way to do that," Plaut said.

But what does Chanukah really teach anyone about being Jewish? That Jews have boring games, cherry *sufganiyot* are disgusting, and singing bear dolls are obnoxious? Even "the miracle of the oil is more a legend than a reality," Plaut said. "The thinness of the theological basis—in some ways, it makes it easier to reach out to the younger generations who might not want that religious depth initially," he said. "Chanukah can be an easy way to celebrate one's Jewish identity without a lot of baggage."

And it's true: Judaism, like any religion, comes with "baggage," whether a Jew grew up Reform, Conservative, Orthodox, or without any observance at all. Jewish identity is complicated even further in interfaith households, which are increasingly common. Doing both Chanukah and Christmas can seem like a cultural compromise for parents feeling familial pressure, and precisely because of its simplicity, Chanukah can seem like an easy entrée into Judaism for kids.

That may be true, but unlike many Jewish holidays, Chanukah doesn't reveal much of what Jewish life is about. It's an empty celebration, and in its lack of substance, it has become filled with literal stuff. "Nobody's buying anything for Yom Kippur . . . other than break-fast food and some bagels," said Neal Hoffman, a former Hasbro employee who invented *Mensch on a Bench*. This, if you haven't heard, is the Jewish alternative to *Elf on a Shelf*, first made in 2013 and now sold in places like Target and Bed Bath & Beyond.

The immaculate conception of *Mensch on a Bench* is, in many ways, the story of contemporary American Judaism. Hoffman is married to a Catholic; his two sons, Jacob and Alex, are being raised Jewish. Around Christmas time, his boys kept asking for trees and presents and the dreaded *Elf on a Shelf*. Hoffman would retort, "Jesus is the meal, Christmas is the dessert. And you can't have dessert if you don't have your dinner." But he didn't want to have to play defense against Christmas; he wanted his kids to have pride in their own cultural heritage. Thus, the Mensch—a stuffed incarnation of the mythical, long-ago Jew who sat on a bench in the Temple and made sure the oil didn't burn down. In three years, Hoffman said, he has sold 120,000 dolls, and his company has started making books even for off-market holidays like Yom Kippur. "The truth is, we lose money on those," he said. "We as Jews have not shown that we want to buy things for other holidays. I don't think that's necessarily bad, that we're keeping the other holidays a little more pure. We're keeping Passover about Seder and keeping Yom Kippur about the fast."

The word he used, *pure*, is telling—even this Chanukah pusher acknowledges that the Festival of Lights is a lesser holiday, fine to adulterate with endless products. It is a low-stakes, low-consequence celebration, and yet for a lot of American Jews, it has probably become one of the few times they encounter their religious culture during the year.

Hoffman, of course, wouldn't sell it that way. For him, the Mensch experience has been one of pride, not just professionally, but for his family. "I have a thousand of my Mensch menorahs in the house. They all have this Try Me button," which produces a little song. "If you've been near a three-year-old, you know that if they see a Try Me button, they'll press it every time," he explained. (Oy, the patience his wife must have—bless her.) "Now I find [my son] walking around by himself, and he's singing the Chanukah prayers year-round, mumbling to himself. I'm so proud of that, so happy about that. That it's all coming from the brand I created—I'm proud of that."

Perhaps this should be enough—it's a Chanukah miracle of its own sort for a three-year-old to slowly start to embrace his Jewish heritage. The holiday may be ridiculous and totally lacking in substance, but "it's part of the joke that we do all this stuff for this unimportant holiday," said Ashton. "We all know what we're doing. We know we're making something grand out of a minor festival because, culturally, we need a much more grand, fun, event" in December.

And besides, griping about Chanukah is a tradition of its own. Every year, Jews kvetch about commercialism, "saying how distasteful it is, or this is completely distorting what this holiday is about," Ashton said. "People have been saying that for more than one hundred years."

2015

Chanukah in a Nineteenth-Century American Home

Esther J. Ruskay

broad, roomy kitchen of a sort not found in modern houses. Half of the wall on one side is taken up by a quaint, old-fashioned bake oven; the remaining space is filled by a large-size modern range. Around the open grate hang long-handled shovels and pokers, and above, on a shelf, rests the coffee roaster, a cylinder of sheet iron, which, turned by the children once a week, sends a delicious fragrance of roasting beans through the house.

Bridget, the servant of fifteen years' standing, has just put away the supper dishes, and, after hanging up the last dish towel, turns and makes a dash for the hearth. "Up wid yez, childern; the Grandmother wants the kitchen tonight to make Chanukah candles." Before they can demur, she has seized, first one pink-toed youngster, then another, and borne them off in triumph, one under each arm, upstairs, where, after tucking them into bed, she listens to them lisp the "*Shema Yisrael*," prompting the sleepy voices and demanding repetition when the familiar words do not sound correct to her devout Catholic ear.

Meanwhile the aspect of the kitchen has changed. Grandmother, with three or four old friends, has taken possession. All of them have been welltried in life's furnace, and have issued therefrom dim as to vision, but clear as to soul; a little strict perhaps in their religious demands upon themselves and the younger people, but full of zeal and love for their faith—so full, indeed, that each day is measured only by the number of good deeds it can hold, of service to the needy and destitute, of ministering to the sick and dying.

Upon a side table lay many balls of soft white twine, which the older boys and girls are twisting into regular lengths, while Grandmother and her cheerful, garrulous friends break the big round cakes of hard yellow wax into small pieces. Later the children help to warm these pieces before the fire, after which, with the length of the kitchen stretching between, they hold the ends of the twine, keeping it taut and stiff while the experienced elders roll the lumps of wax about the twine.

Very gently the aged palms work, and mold the wax that must be free from flaws and impurities, for were not the Maccabees and their victorious hosts careful, before dedicating the Temple, which had been spoiled by the Syrians, that only the purest oil should be used to celebrate their victory? And when the twine is covered evenly and smoothly along its whole polished yellow length, *clip*, *clip*, *clip*, go the scissors next to the yardstick measured against the thin golden line, and *clip*, *clip*, again into smaller and still smaller sizes, after which the young people gather them together in even heaps, tying them into neat bundles of forty-four, bundles which are subsequently to be presented to friends far and near for the home celebration of Chanukah.

On the first night of Chanukah, each child is presented with a funny little top, called a trendel, which he may twirl around sharply, and watch as it spins itself out. It is sure to fall with one of its sides uppermost, and as each side bears a raised Hebrew letter, the fun of the game hinges upon which letter the player turns up to view.

Such were some of the preparations for what was to be to young and old among the descendants of the Maccabee warriors a glad festival week. After this followed days of cleaning and refurbishing, of baking and cooking; for most certainly a whole week of games, of music and song, of gathering together of the various family clans could not well be lived through without an abundance of the good things of life. In all these pleasures the children were allowed their full share.

Nor were the poor forgotten. Fortunate winners in any of the games of chance (which, by the way, because fully permitted and enjoyed during this one week of Chanukah, never suggested themselves as an indulgence during the rest of the year) were compelled to put half of their winnings into the boxes fastened upon the inside of the closet door, the one marked *Palestine*, the contents of which were taken out twice a year and sent to Zion, the other for the home poor.

Each evening, after the lighting of the candles, the children's tuneful voices mingled with the deeper ones of the elders in the grand old harmony of the Chanukah hymn; and before the tiny wax tapers had begun to burn down in their sockets, and even while the *shamash* was still sending up his sputtering appreciation of his position in front, the children, helped and abetted by the older folks, entered upon an evening of such unrestricted enjoyment and pleasant family intercourse as is rarely witnessed in these too-busy and too-enlightened days.

1902

The Coming of Light

Mark Strand

Even this late it happens:
the coming of love, the coming of light.
You wake and the candles are lit as if by themselves,
stars gather, dreams pour into your pillows,
sending up warm bouquets of air.
Even this late the bones of the body shine
and tomorrow's dust flares into breath.

1979

The Chanukah Light

I. L. Peretz

My topcoat was already in my hand, and yet I could not decide: to go, or not to go—to give my lesson! Oh, it is so unpleasant outside, such horrible weather!—a mile's trudge—and then what?

"Once more: *pakad, pakadti*"—once more, conjugating the Hebrew verb "to visit": the old housemaster, who has got through his sixty and odd years of life without knowing any grammar; who has been ten times to Leipzig, two or three times to Danzig; who once all but landed in Constantinople—and who cannot understand such waste of money: Grammar, indeed? A fine bargain!

Then the young housemaster, who allows that it is far more practical to wear earlocks, a fur cap, and a braided caftan, to consult with a "good Jew," and not to know any grammar . . . not that he is anything but otherwise than orthodox himself . . . but he is obliged, as a merchant, to mix with men, to wear a hat and a stiff shirt; to permit his wife to visit the theater; his daughter, to read books; and to engage a tutor for his son . . .

"My father, of course, knows best! But one must move with the times!" He cannot make up his mind to be left in the lurch by the times! "I only beg of you," he said to me, "don't make an unbeliever of the boy! I will give you," he said, "as much as would pay for a whole lot of grammar, if you will *not* teach him that the earth goes around the sun!"

And I promised that he should never hear it from me, because—because this was my only lesson, and I had a sick mother at home!

To go, or not to go?

The whole family will be present to watch me when I give my lesson.

She also?

She sits in the background, always deep in a book; now and again she lifts her long, silken lashes, and a little brightness is diffused through the room; but so seldom, so seldom!

And what is to come of it?

Nothing ever *can* come of it, except heartache.

"Listen!" My mother's weak voice from the bed recalls me to myself. "The Feldscher says, if only I had a pair of warm, woolen socks, I might creep about the room a little!"

That, of course, decides it.

Except for the lady of the house, who has gone to the play, as usual without the knowledge of her father-in-law, I find the whole family assembled round the pinchbeck samovar. The young housemaster acknowledges my greeting with a negligent "a good year to you!" and goes on turning over in his palm a pack of playing cards. Doubtless he expects company.

The old housemaster, in a peaked cap and a voluminous Turkish dressing gown, does not consider it worthwhile to remove from his lips the long pipe with its amber mouthpiece, or to lift his eyes from off his well-worn book of devotions. He merely gives me a nod, and once more sinks his attention in the portion appointed for Chanukah.

She also is intent on her reading, only *her* book, as usual, is a novel.

My arrival makes a disagreeable impression on my pupil.

"Oh, I say!" and he springs up from his seat at the table, and lowers his black-ringed, little head defiantly, "lessons today?"

"Why not?" smiles his father.

"But it's Chanukah!" answers the boy, tapping the floor with his foot, and pointing to the first light, which has been placed in the window, behind the curtain, and fastened to a bit of wood.

"Quite right!" growls the old gentleman.

"Well, well," says the younger one, with indifference, "you must excuse him for once!"

I have an idea that *she* has become suddenly paler, that she bends lower over her book.

I wish them all good night, but the young housemaster will not let me go.

"You must stay to tea!"

"And poppy seed cake!" cries my pupil, joyfully. He is quite willing to be friends, so long as there is no question of conjugating "*pakad, pakadti.*"

I am diffident as to accepting, but the boy seizes my hand, and, with a roguish smile on his restless features, he places a chair for me opposite to his sister's.

Has he observed anything? On *my* side, of course, I mean . . .

She is always abstracted and lost in her reading. Very likely she looks upon me as an idler, or even worse . . . she does not know that I have a sick mother at home!

"It will soon be time for you to dress!" exclaims her father, impatiently.

"Soon, very soon, Tatishe!" she answers hastily, and her pale cheeks take a tinge of color.

The young housemaster abandons himself once more to his reflections; my pupil sends a top spinning across the table; the old man lays down his book, and stretches out a hand for his tea.

Involuntarily I glance at the Chanukah light opposite to me in the window.

It burns so sadly, so low, as if ashamed in the presence of the great silvered lamp hanging over the dining table, and lighting so brilliantly the elegant tea service.

I feel more depressed than ever, and do not observe that she is offering me a glass of tea.

"With lemon?" her melancholy voice rouses me.

"Perhaps you prefer milk?" says her father.

"Look out! The milk is smoked!" cries my pupil, warningly.

An exclamation escapes her:

"How can you be so . . . !"

Silence once more. Nothing but a sound of sipping and a clink of spoons. Suddenly my pupil is moved to inquire:

"After all, teacher, what *is* Chanukah?"

"Ask the rabbi tomorrow in school!" says the old man, impatiently.

"Eh!" is the prompt reply, "I should think a tutor knew better than a rabbi!"

The old man casts an angry glance at his son, as if to say: "Do you see?"

"*I* want to know about Chanukah, too!" she exclaims softly.

"Well, well," says the young housemaster to me, "let us hear your version of Chanukah by all means!"

"It happened," I begin, "in the days when the Greeks oppressed us in the land of Israel. The Greeks—" But the old man interrupts me with a sour look:

"In the Benedictions it says: 'The wicked kingdom of Javan.'"

"It comes to the same thing," observes his son, "what *we* call Javan, *they* call Greeks."

"The Greeks," I resume, "oppressed us terribly! It was our darkest hour. As a nation, we were threatened with extinction. After a few ill-starred risings, the life seemed to be crushed out of us, the last gleam of hope had faded. Although in our own country, we were trodden under foot like worms."

The young housemaster has long ceased to pay me any attention. His ear is turned to the door; he is intent on listening for the arrival of a guest.

But the old housemaster fixes me with his eye, and, when I have a second time used the word "oppressed," he can no longer contain himself:

"A man should be explicit! 'Oppressed'—what does that convey to me? They forced us to break the Sabbath; they forbade us to keep our festivals, to study the Law, even to practice circumcision."

"Do you play 'Preference'?" inquires the younger gentleman, suddenly, "or perhaps even poker?"

Once more there is silence, and I continue: "The misfortune was aggravated by the fact that the nobility and the wealthy began to feel ashamed of their own people, and to adopt Greek ways of living. They used to frequent the gymnasiums."

She and the old gentleman look at me in astonishment.

"In the gymnasiums of those days," I hasten to add, "there was no studying—they used to practice gymnastics, naked, men and women together—"

The two pairs of eyes lower their gaze, but the young housemaster raises his with a flash.

"*What* did you say?"

I make no reply, but go on to speak of the theaters where men fought wild beasts and oxen, and of other Greek manners and customs that must have been contrary to Jewish tradition.

"The Greeks thought nothing of all this; they were bent on effacing every trace of independent national existence. They set up an altar in the street with an *Avodah Zarah*, and commanded us to sacrifice to it."

"What is that?" she asks in Polish.

I explain; and the old man adds excitedly:

"And a swine, too! We were to sacrifice a swine to it!"

"And there was found a Jew to approach the altar with an offering.

"But that same day, the old Maccabeus, with his five sons, had come down from the hills, and before the Greek soldiers could intervene, the miserable apostate was lying in his blood, and the altar was torn down. In one second the rebellion was ablaze. The Maccabees, with a handful of men, drove out the far more numerous Greek garrisons. The people were set free!

"It is that victory we celebrate with our poor, little illumination, with our Chanukah lights."

"What?" and the old man, trembling with rage, springs out of his chair. "*That* is the Chanukah light? Come here, wretched boy!" he screams to his grandson, who, instead of obeying, shrinks from him in terror.

The old man brings his fist down on the table, so that the glasses ring.

"It means—when we had driven out the unclean sons of Javan, there was only one little cruse of holy olive oil left . . ."

But a fit of coughing stops his breath, and his son hastens up, and assists him into the next room.

I wish to leave, but she detains me.

"You are against assimilation, then?" she asks.

"To assimilate," I reply, "is to consume, to eat, to digest. We assimilate beef and bread, and others wish to assimilate *us*—to eat us up like bread and meat."

She is silent for a few seconds, and then she asks anxiously:

"But will there always, always be wars and dissensions between the nations?"

"Oh no!" I answer, "on one point they *must* all agree—in the end."

"And that is?"

"Humanity. When each is free to follow his own bent, then they will all agree."

She is lost in thought, she has more to say, but there comes a tap at the door—

"Mamma!" she exclaims under her breath, and escapes, after giving me her hand—for the first time!

ON THE NEXT DAY but one, while I was still in bed, I received a letter by the postman.

The envelope bore the name of her father's firm: "Jacob Berenholz."

My heart beat like a sledgehammer. Inside there were only ten rubles—my pay for the month that was not yet complete.

Goodbye, lessons!

1906

The Last Hour

David Frischmann

Outside the wind wails and shrieks. The rain sweeps upon the roofs and beats upon the windowpanes. But within, the house is full of light and joy, radiating in every corner, glowing in every heart. Upon the silver Chanukah menorah there shines the eighth candle tonight, and opposite it the waxen *shamash* stands bent and molten, its fire flickering and dying.

In the tapestried armchair Grandmother sits, attired in her comeliest garments, garments worn on Sabbaths and on holidays. Her eyes are bright with happiness. The folds of her silken shawl fall from her head; her jeweled earrings sparkle and send little lightnings from beneath her ears. All of us gathered about her and I on her footstool, my head resting on her knees, entranced; she sits, in profound thought, her lips shut, only her eyes gleaming with inspired light. Truly the secrets of God are hidden in those eyes, full of wisdom and eternally bright! Her forehead is infinitely wrinkled; her back is bent, almost humped; her hands quiver, her very voice quivers—but her eyes, they are young, they are eternally bright!

Silence! From her cloud of dreams she raises her heavy, weary head. "My children, I am old and gray, am I not? My days outnumber the sands on the shore of the sea and my nights defy computation, but the words which I am about to tell you this evening are even older than I am myself, older than myself by thousands of years, and I, my dear children, must tell you these words which fill my heart even to overflowing."

Outside the wind still wails and shrieks in an eerie voice. But the voice of Grandmother rises above the cry of the wind. She speaks:

"My children, you are expecting, no doubt, that I will tell you of the miracle of Chanukah. That is your error. The story of Chanukah and the deeds of Antiochus you have heard long ago. I have it in mind, however, to tell you of that which took place in Jerusalem in the reign of Antiochus five or six years before the miracle of Chanukah. It is the tale of a little Hebrew lad who came to *heder* one day and began bitterly to cry, not because he was being beaten there, forsooth, but because there was an aching in his heart and in his soul an anguish. Truly these words are full of sorrow and great bitterness."

And Grandmother is suddenly silent. Her eyelids slowly droop as in a dream. And I, all anticipation, sit on her footstool, my head resting on her knees.

THE STREETS OF JERUSALEM. Rays of sweetness and light pour from heaven upon the goodly dwellings of Israel. From horizon to horizon the sky extends, a perfect blue, save for bits of clouds slowly wandering above like travelers spent with journeying. A clear warm breeze gently rustles the leaves. This summer is verily a warm one—this summer of the year 3590 of the divine creation.

In the street the children romp and play. They are happy; they laugh; they sing. Beneath their feet the golden sand is scattered; above their heads there burns a golden sun. Their hearts swell with happiness. Of a sudden, they hear the shout of the crier: "'Tis time, my children, to go to your studies. Hurry then, hurry to the *heder*." As suddenly the children stop and look hither and thither. A tall old man stands before them. His beard is white and falls upon his chest, and his eyes gleam as he looks upon them with a despairing bitterness. Who does not know this ancient graybeard? Who does not recognize Rabbi Jose, the son of Joezer, of the city of Tzeradoh?

As he stands there and stares at them a kindly contentment shines from his face; on his eyelashes there cling large tears. "These are the remnants of Judah," he mutters to himself, "and this is the staff upon which our nation is to lean. The young ones are still ours." As one entranced he stands there, stands and dreams in the drowsiness of summer.

What had befallen his people in these latter days? True it was that they were living in the land of Israel, yet the land was not Israel's. This country was now subject to the whims of the Greek Antiochus Epiphanes, who at this time was carrying on his military expeditions in Egypt, while the wicked Andronicus was sent to Palestine to fill his place as governor. This tyrant was now reigning with a mighty hand, seeking to root out the last spirit of Judaism which still lingered in abandoned corners, and to plant in its stead a spirit of Hellenism. By converting Jewish customs into Greek and by setting up Greek gods he was slowly but surely spreading that spirit over the land. The streets of Jerusalem ceased to be called by their Hebrew names; Greek ones were assigned instead. Hebrew coins went out of circulation; Greek currency took its place. Hebrew names disappeared; Jews were known by Greek cognomens. Hebrew flags waved no more from the public buildings; Greek ones fluttered vauntingly upon their poles. Even from the courthouse of the Sanhedrin they took the Hebrew standard and hung a Greek one in its stead. The high priest, who still strove for the ideals of his nation, was replaced; and his office given to Menelaus, a man of heathen inclinations.

"Still are the young ones left to us, still are the sucklings of the kindergarten ours," he says, and again his face is filled with bitterness and again he cries: "To the heder, children, to the heder."

In compliance, the young boys hasten in all directions, and little Joezer, the youngest son of Rabbi Jose, follows them eagerly. With such a sun shining in all its splendor it is no light thing to leave the open air beneath the blue sky to shut oneself up in a heder. With merry hearts the young lads cross the bridge of Kedron. They stop near a Greek toyshop. Little Joezer gazes into its show window, transfixed, as if his feet were nailed to the spot. Suddenly there appears upon the threshold of the shop a Greek slave. He yells at the boy in a shrill, angry voice. Young Joezer runs with all his might, and stops to look neither to right nor to left. He passes the farm of Jehoshaphat, the bridge of Antiochus, and the fields of the washers, till he comes to the market of Andronicus. Here he stops for a while and wistfully regards the souvenirs sold by the Greeks, toys and talismans brought from Athens and from Sparta and from Byzantium. Here are golden sandals, chains of pearls, silver stars, and here images of horses and of dogs and of man, wrought in wood and stone, works of an artist. And all these things glitter and gleam in the sun and are pleasing to the eye. All at once he recalls that he is in a hurry and that he must go to the heder. When he comes to the open land which lies behind the Temple he halts. Here in the northwestern portion a gymnasium had been erected, where the Greeks taught the Hebrews all forms of acrobatics and the art of fighting. The boy stood enraptured at the sight of young Hebrews exercising themselves in the open air. How good it must be to be thus always under the warmth of the sun and in the coolness of the breeze, he thought. Two Hebrew boys enter the ring, and quick of hand and fleet of foot, they engage in a spirited struggle, each attempting to vanquish the other, and after some time, both falling to the ground, the surrounding crowd lustily cheering the Hebrew champions. There next enters the ring a Hebrew lad, naked to the waist, who begins to dance with all the charm and perfection of the art, while the lyre and the drum emphasize his motion. Happiness and joy is everywhere. Only upon the heart of Joezer, of little Joezer, does there come a pang of sorrow, for he has remembered that he must hurry to heder. But his feet are as glued to the place; he stands there transfixed, his eyes do not leave the ring. This is new youth, he thinks, these are new games, new sports, new joys. His evil spirit, however, does not allow him to leave this spot. Already four hours have passed, and still the lad is watching the sports in the gymnasium. The sun has already climbed to its central height in the heavens. And a great terror possesses little Joezer. Half a day is already gone, and he has not yet been to heder. What will be the words, the sharp, bitter words that his teacher will fling at him? What will be his warm reception? And already he imagines the severe words of the rabbi and already he sees his angry face, and already he hears his harsh voice. He rouses himself from his trance, and runs, runs.

And as he runs there follow him visions that he had beheld in the gymnasium—boys and girls, half naked, seem to pursue him. The dances and the combats, the exercises and the acrobatics, the music of the lyre and the beat of the drum are again with him. And from all these remembered sounds there rises louder and sterner the voice of his rabbi, scolding and wrathful. He hurries faster and faster, his feet do not seem to touch the ground; he is already in the street of the heder. His heart pounds violently, he stops for a moment before the door of the heder to rest and wipe the perspiration from his brow. So silent it is that he hears the beating of his heart. A second passes—and his hand is on the doorknob. Another—and he is already within the classroom. A great terror and darkness fall upon him, and his legs are weighty as with lead. What is this? A silence as of death reigns today in the classroom. A spirit of mourning, of speechless mourning, pervades the whole room. The boys sit silent and motionless. No one says a word, no one even winks an eyelash. Truly the heder is different today from what it was yesterday. Even the rabbi stands leaning upon the desk—his brow wrinkled and resting upon the palm of his hand, his eyes shut. Suddenly he raises his head, and his eyes catch sight of little Joezer. "My son, you are late this morning, very late, but you did good in coming, even if late."

Could it be? His voice was soft and kind, softer than poured oil, and his words full of compassion and regret, words that fall deeply into the heart of little Joezer. When did his rabbi last speak to him in this fashion? Whence came this voice, so full of bitterness and sorrow and yet so full of warmth and pity? At this very moment the conscience of the little boy hurt him for having wasted the whole morning, for having come late. "My son," continues the rabbi, his voice quivering, "my son, take your book and study your lesson, for ere you will know it this hour will be the last . . . tomorrow we cease to learn Hebrew." His voice is choked with tears . . . all the boys in the heder shudder and commiserate with their rabbi, an old man weeping like a child. "Our last fire they have quenched, our language they have taken from us and what will we now teach our children? How will they now be able to know the spirit and the splendor and the greatness of their people?"

He passes his hand over his eyes; he weeps; the children weep. And in this silence and sorrow little Joezer finds himself bewildered: his heart beats loudly, and in that moment a new spirit had come into him, a new soul had entered into him.

"So this, my children, is our last hour. Tomorrow we cease to study our language." The voice of the rabbi is heard a third time, but it is a voice no longer filled with bitterness and sorrow, but with softness and pure compassion—a voice which seems to say: "Tomorrow all existence will fade from off the face of the earth and only wilderness will reign instead."

The young boys take their books and hasten home. And as young Joezer takes his books, his hands quiver and his eyes are washed with tears. Never up to this day did he understand his lesson so well, never up to this day did the words of the rabbi sink so deeply in his heart. On this day one of the world's languages will be borne to the grave; on this day a nation will be lost among the nations; on this day a land will perish from among the lands. And the young lad, in his heart, knows and understands these things. And as his rabbi speaks to him these words of kindness and warmth, his voice sweet and pleasant, his explanations clear and memorable, they are like secrets of God emanating from the square letters, whose like he had never heard nor seen before. Then did the lad make an inward vow never to step within the Grecian gymnasium.

The sun has set. Within the heder the darkness has cast its shadows into every corner and nothing is heard save the voice of the rabbi trembling as he studies the Law of God this last, last hour.

Outside before the door of the heder is heard the voice of the passing men, loudly speaking Greek, and the whole street seems full of joy and happiness . . .

THE LIGHT IN THE CHANUKAH menorah has long since flickered out. In the armchair Grandmother sits; her hands cover her eyes; she is silent. She has ended her story—outside the wind has long since ceased its wailing and its shrieking, but in the house there are shadows and silence and sorrow.

His Wife, His Latkes, and His Friend Peysekh-Moyshe

B. Kovner

A former boss of mine, a recent widower, told it to me like this:

"My friend Peysekh-Moyshe? First of all, he's a *galitsyaner*. Second of all, a vegetarian. He won't eat any meat, any fish, not even a piece of herring, nothing that comes from any sort of living creature. And third of all, he's one of those fired-up warriors against the institution of marriage.

"Only a fool . . . or an ass," he liked to say, "would ever get married."

He thinks marriage is the world's greatest tragedy, even worse than war.

"How can a man take a strange girl he doesn't know the first thing about and promise to keep her fed for an entire lifetime?""

If you saw my friend, you'd swear he'd just gotten out of the hospital—pale, skinny, sad, and hungry. Not that this gets in the way of his good looks.

Peysekh-Moyshe doesn't know the meaning of the word "work": he can't do it, he won't do it, he doesn't have it. If they were giving out jobs *not* to work, he'd get hired in a second. And you know how it goes. If you don't work, you don't have any money, and if you don't have any money, you don't have any clothes or food. He goes around in rags, every day a fast.

Occasionally, a fellow immigrant will lend him a few cents. He'll buy a bunch of figs and eat, counting down his days and his meals fig by fig. And if he happens to meet up with another vegetarian who's also looking for something to chew on, then each of them enjoys a fig.

IT WAS LAST CHANUKAH. The third night, I believe. A cold evening. You could hear the frost cracking and the dry wind howling strange songs in concert with the freshly fallen snow when I bumped into my friend the vegetarian on Pitkin Avenue, in Brownsville. He was standing outside a restaurant blowing into his fists.

"Hello there!" I called out to him cheerfully. "What are you standing around here for? Come up to my place for a little while. The house is warm! You'll drink a little tea, get a bite to eat. Come!"

"Thank you kindly, but I would prefer not to," replied my friend. "Leave me be, don't force the issue."

But I couldn't just leave him behind and so brought him back home with me.

The house was bright and clean, warm and happy. My wife—my wife is gorgeous—was standing by the hot stove in a white apron, frying up latkes in goose fat. The latkes sizzled and sputtered, muttering from the pan. Their scent filled the house. My wife's cheeks were a fiery red, her eyes sparkled, her chest heaved—a vision of beauty! Good-naturedly, she offered our guest her hand and told him to take a seat.

Soon the table was covered with gefilte fish, a whole roast goose, and a huge platter of hot, fragrant latkes. My wife sat down next to Peysekh-Moyshe and told him not to be shy. "Eat as much as your heart desires!" she said to him. "There's enough for everyone. Eat up, make yourself at home!"

"I simply can't . . . I mustn't . . ." my poor friend replied. "It's against our principles . . . It's . . ."

"Never mind your principles!" my wife interrupted. "First eat your supper. Then we'll drink a glass of tea, shuffle up a few rounds of Sixty-Six, and *then* we can chat about your principles . . ." As she was talking, my wife gave him a playful little pat on the shoulder . . .

After a short moment of internal philosophical wrangling, Peysekh-Moyshe surrendered. Before doing anything else, he pushed his chair closer to my wife's. Then he poured himself a shot and threw himself into the feast. But not all food is created equal! He stuffed both cheeks. After the fish—a second shot; then a whole quarter goose—and another shot; then soup with kasha with yet another shot—until at last, latkes with tea.

You could say that he didn't even chew the latkes, but swallowed them whole, like swallowing a pill! Woe unto the latke that fell into his mouth!

Then the three of us sat down to play cards. The whole time, he couldn't stop throwing glances at my wife. She wasn't exactly stingy with her smile either. He was in seventh heaven. Pure bliss!

THIS STORY HAS a very unhappy ending. He spent the night at our place. He got up in the morning, ate breakfast, lunch, and dinner, and slept over once more. Then again: he got up in the morning, ate his fill, and slept through the night— and so on and so forth week after week. Around Purim, when the weather started getting warmer, he ran away with my wife and—*poof!* Gone without a trace!

1914

The Feast of Lights

Emma Lazarus

Kindle the taper like the steadfast star
Ablaze on evening's forehead o'er the earth,
And add each night a lustre till afar
An eightfold splendor shine above thy hearth.
Clash, Israel, the cymbals, touch the lyre,
Blow the brass trumpet and the harsh-tongued horn;
Chant psalms of victory till the heart takes fire,
The Maccabean spirit leap new-born.

Remember how from wintry dawn till night,
Such songs were sung in Zion, when again
On the high altar flamed the sacred light,
And, purified from every Syrian stain,
The foam-white walls with golden shields were hung,
With crowns and silken spoils, and at the shrine,
Stood, midst their conqueror-tribe, five chieftains sprung
From one heroic stock, one seed divine.

Five branches grown from Mattathias' stem,
The Blessed John, the Keen-Eyed Jonathan,
Simon the fair, the Burst-of Spring, the Gem,

Eleazar, Help of-God; o'er all his clan
Judas the Lion-Prince, the Avenging Rod,
Towered in warrior-beauty, uncrowned king,
Armed with the breastplate and the sword of God,
Whose praise is: "He received the perishing."

They who had camped within the mountain-pass,
Couched on the rock, and tented neath the sky,
Who saw from Mizpah's heights the tangled grass
Choke the wide Temple-courts, the altar lie
Disfigured and polluted—who had flung
Their faces on the stones, and mourned aloud
And rent their garments, wailing with one tongue,
Crushed as a wind-swept bed of reeds is bowed,

Even they by one voice fired, one heart of flame,
Though broken reeds, had risen, and were men,
They rushed upon the spoiler and o'ercame,
Each arm for freedom had the strength of ten.
Now is their mourning into dancing turned,
Their sackcloth doffed for garments of delight,
Week-long the festive torches shall be burned,
Music and revelry wed day with night.

Still ours the dance, the feast, the glorious Psalm,
The mystic lights of emblem, and the Word.
Where is our Judas? Where our five-branched palm?
Where are the lion-warriors of the Lord?
Clash, Israel, the cymbals, touch the lyre,
Sound the brass trumpet and the harsh-tongued horn,
Chant hymns of victory till the heart take fire,
The Maccabean spirit leap new-born!

1882

Roller Coaster

Gila Green

Miriam was too late getting down the stairs. By the time she made it into the living room it was over. She could only look from her son to her husband. Shock parachuted into the room like an invisible enemy.

That's not completely true. The whole truth hurts Miriam's stomach and she skips over it in the retelling, even to herself; the shame is too great. The truth is she had made it into the living room to witness her husband, Beni, enraged. His hand clutched her son's iPod high in the air.

Smash! The first hit divided the iPod in two. Beni bent down, snatched the largest piece and hurled it to the floor, where it broke into still more pieces. He repeated the action of seeking out the largest piece and destroying it until there was nothing left, but tooth-sized plastic bits. Miriam brought her hands to her cheeks, but sound was trapped in her throat.

She knew that she should never have left the two of them alone, not even for a breath, not even because they had five children all younger than eleven who needed her, too. It wasn't enough of an excuse. When would she learn?

In the morning the family had decided on an outing to SuperLand, an amusement park in Rishon LeZion. The schools were closed for the Chanukah holidays and it was common for parents to take off work, too. Family time. They had to leave early if they were going to make it back for sunset, the optimal time for lighting Chanukah candles. The earlier candles are lit after sunset, the more time left for passersby to be reminded of light that can spring out of the darkness at any moment.

It still astounds Miriam how her mind surrounds the memory of that night with minute details: the warm, sunny winter weather; the crawling traffic on their way home; how she'd returned from candle-lighting on their front lawn to find that the dog had leaped onto the table and eaten the dinner they'd agonized over for an hour, before finally agreeing on a menu.

"What happened?" Miriam finally coughed out two words.

"Your fourteen-year-old got in line for the roller coaster and started talking to some secular girl in a miniskirt. They exchanged phone numbers and already became friends on Facebook. Is this why we take him on family outings? To meet *pritzus*? He broke the family rule. We do not start up with girls and certainly not ones from who knows where. She could be from any kind of home and he invites it into ours. For all we know she's one of those nutcases we read about who get boys to befriend her on the internet and then meets them somewhere and has them kidnapped or killed."

"She talked to me. I didn't talk to her. There's no law against talking to girls. So, she's not religious, so what? She's not some stupid spy. Dad is nuts. Crazy. I can be friends on Facebook with anyone I want. And what do girls have to do with breaking my things? That iPod was a present for my bar mitzvah. You didn't buy it. I had all of my personal things on there. My pictures. My memories. He just grabbed it out of my hand. And if I smashed *his* iPhone, he'd freak out. I'm never speaking to him again! I hate him."

BUT MIRIAM HEARD her son's voice only after all of the menorahs were packed away next to the dreidels and leftover candles. After she'd finally dialed the right number and found him at a friend's. She had tried to turn her words into a soothing plaster, "Come home."

The silence that filled the house after their son disappeared broke only after three long family days with the children, nutritious homemade vegetable soups for dinner to balance out the fried potato pancakes and chocolate coin-shaped candies. After sunset Miriam did not look at Beni, neither during the candle-lighting, nor over the recitation of the Hebrew blessings.

While her children sang holiday songs with her husband and spun their dreidels for marshmallows, Miriam watched the light flicker in the windowpane. She tried to accept that she was a mother who did not know where her son was and had not known for a while, but it was like trying to accept an incoming missile. She blinded herself to her son's smaller menorah that sat unlit in the window, cold and uncared for.

They lit one large family menorah together, but Jewish boys over the age of thirteen were considered adults, and last year Beni had proudly purchased a second one in gleaming silver, which he insisted now on leaving unused in the window until the last day of the holiday was over, as though the candelabrum could reach out its eight arms and gather their son home.

In the dark, when the glow from the candles had long faded and the house slept, Miriam reviewed the scene. There had been nothing in the agonizingly slow car ride back from Rishon LeZion to Jerusalem to indicate what was coming—no narrow looks or change in atmosphere. Still, she berated herself for not sensing something in her husband's body language. If she had, maybe her son wouldn't have slipped through her fingers like the last moments of a dream.

After their son's departure, Beni had eyed her with fury, as though *she* had picked up a teenaged girl in a low-cut top and miniskirt in Rishon LeZion's only amusement park. She knew he was waiting for her to assert he had done the right thing, that they couldn't allow their son to pick up loose girls in front of their very eyes, to expose this immodesty to his little sisters. But she couldn't black out her husband's arm, cutting through the air with all of his might and, in mental replay, she heard her son's cry as his iPod burst open on the tiled floor. She absorbed Beni's fury into her heart, where it began to dig a hole, and said nothing.

Miriam counted her blessings: Beni had swept up the pieces of their son's prized possession, sparing her at least that. Not one of her children had heard what was going on downstairs in the living room, or the front door slamming hard enough to sway the flames that were burning inside the glass box they used to surround the menorah, to keep it safe from extinguishing too early on the front lawn.

For the rest of the holiday, Miriam and Beni spent every moment with their younger children, answering their whims for ice cream, for another outing, for just one more video before bed. Their son's cell phone might as well have been smashed to pieces, too.

On the eighth night, Miriam's breathing changed rhythm when Elazar answered.

"I'm not speaking to dad until he buys me a new iPod."

"I'm not buying him anything until the boy demonstrates that he understands why I broke it."

The angry words flap around her head whenever a friend or neighbor asks: How was your holiday? But she can't reveal them. They burn. So, she buries them inside of herself, in the hole next to Beni's fury, the way her son buries the digital photographs of the girl in the white miniskirt and low-cut top behind a Facebook code he thinks she doesn't know.

2012

Miracles for a Broken Planet

Chaim Potok

Chanukah is the Festival of Lights. It commemorates an ancient Jewish rebellion against oppression, during which the Temple in Jerusalem was miraculously recaptured from pagan Hellenizers and rededicated to the worship of God. The candles of Chanukah celebrate that rededication. They also help brighten the long winter nights.

But I remember a Chanukah when darkness almost overpowered the light.

It was the first week of November 1938. The final years of the Depression lay like a polluting mist across the streets of New York. On afternoons when it did not rain, I would play on the sidewalk in front of the plate glass window of the candy store near our apartment house. The bubble of darkness on the other side of the world bumped only vaguely against my consciousness. I was very young then, interested more in Flash Gordon and Buck Rogers than Adolf Hitler.

One afternoon I was near the candy store, in the cardboard box that was my rocket ship, when an elderly couple walked slowly by; I caught some of their frightened words. Before supper that evening I saw my mother standing over the kitchen sink, her head bowed and heard her whispering agitatedly to herself. Later, my father came home from work, drenched in weariness; he turned on the radio and became wearier still.

That night I lay awake in my bed and saw the pieces of the day come together and form a portrait of terror.

A Jewish boy had shot a German, the old people had said. We will pay dearly for it, very dearly.

The boy had been sent by his parents to live with his uncle in Paris, my father had murmured. Then his parents were deported to Poland. The boy went out of his mind, my mother had said in a voice full of fear. He did not know what he was doing.

He wanted to kill the German ambassador, my father had said. He wanted the world to know about the suffering of Germany's Jews. Inside the embassy, he made a mistake and shot and wounded a subordinate instead.

He was out of his head with grief, my mother had said. He could not have known what he was doing.

I lay very still in my bed, thinking of the boy who had shot the German and wondering what the Germans would do to the Jews. Two days later the subordinate died.

In the weeks that followed I dreamed about the synagogues that were burning all over Germany, about the Jews who were being sent to concentration camps, about the looted stores and smashed shop windows. One day I stood in front of our apartment house and imagined our street littered with glass, shattered glass everywhere, the plate glass window of the candy store splattered across the sidewalk, the store itself burned and gutted. I imagined the entire block, the neighborhood, the city heaped with broken glass and thick with the stench of fire. The days of that November and December began to go dark, until it seemed all the world would soon be shades of darkness: dark sun and dark moon, dark sky and dark earth, dark night and dark day. I was a child then, but I still remember that darkness as a malevolence I could touch and smell, an evil growth draining my world of its light.

My world seemed thick with that darkness when Chanukah came that year on the twenty-fifth of December.

I remember my father chanting the blessings over the first candle on the first night of the festival. He was short and balding; and he chanted in a thin, intense voice. I stood between him and my mother, gazing at the flame of the first night's candle. The flame seemed pitiful against the malignant darkness outside our window. I went to bed and was cold with dread over the horror of the world.

The next night two candles were lighted. Again my father chanted the blessing before the lighting and the prayer that follows, when the candles are burning: "We kindle these lights on account of the miracles, the deliverances, and the wonders which You did for our fathers . . . During eight days of Chanukah these lights are sacred . . . We are only to look at them, in order that we may give thanks unto Your name for Your miracles, Your deliverances and Your wonders."

I wanted a miracle. But there were no miracles during that Chanukah. Where was God? I kept dreaming of burning synagogues.

On the eighth and final night of the festival I stood with my parents in front of the burning candles. The darkness mocked their light. I could see my parents glancing at me. My mother sighed. Then my father murmured my name.

"You want another miracle?" he asked wearily.

I did not respond.

"Yes," he said. "You want another miracle." He was silent a moment. Then he said, in a gentle, urging voice, "I also want another miracle. But if it does not come, we will make a human miracle. We will give the world the special gifts of our Jewishness. We will not let the world burn out our souls."

The candles glowed feebly against the dark window.

"Sometimes I think man is a greater miracle maker than God," my father said tiredly, looking at the candles. "God does not have to live day after day on this broken planet. Perhaps you will learn to make your own miracles. I will try to teach you how to make human miracles."

I lay awake a long time that night and did not believe my father could ever teach me that. But now, decades later, I think he taught me well. And I am trying hard to teach it to my own children.

1972

The Miraculous Oil

Caroline Deutsch

Little cruet in the Temple
That doest feed the sacrificial flame,
What a true expressive symbol
Art thou of my race, of Israel's fame!
Thou for days the oil didst furnish
To illume the Temple won from foe—
So for centuries in my people
Spirit of resistance ne'er burnt low.
It was cast from home and country,
Gloom and sorrow were its daily lot;
Yet the torch of faith gleamed steady,
Courage, like thy oil, forsook it not.
Mocks and jeers were all its portion,
Death assailed it in ten thousand forms—
Yet this people never faltered,
Hope, its beacon, led it through all storms.
Poorer than dumb, driven cattle,
It went forth enslaved from its estate,
All its footsore wand'rings lighted
By its consciousness of worth innate.

Luckless fortunes could not bend it;
Unjust laws increased its wondrous faith;
From its heart, exhaustless streaming,
Freedom's light shone on its thorny path.
Oil that burnt in olden Temple,
Eight days only didst thou give forth light!
Oil of faith sustained its people
Through the centuries of darkest night!

Circa 1892

Judah the Maccabee

Jacob Fichman

I

THE WHITE DONKEY with skinny legs bore his young rider on his back along the narrow slope that winds between the mountains of Judea on the road from Jerusalem to Modi'in, shuddering from time to time at his master's frequent blows, but leaping gloomily with clipped ears from hillock to hillock and rock to rock, utterly stunned at his master's fury as well as the heat of the day. He was not used to such rough treatment and couldn't make out what had come over the beguiling youth who just the day before yesterday, as they went up to the great city of stone that sat in the mountains, had been in a wonderful mood, and stroked his neck all the way fondly, while his mouth never stopped singing out loud. Yet today he'd bothered his rest at dawn in the stables where the trough had yet to be filled with rich fodder, and before even giving him a crust of breakfast they went out alone from the city teeming with men and many beasts, and since morning had been beating and urging him on the steeps and on inclines, without letting him catch his breath even a little on the wearisome mountain road.

Truly a different spirit had come over the young rider, who'd gone out the day before yesterday with his townsfolk from Modi'in mountain, to see Jerusalem, the capital of Judea, for the first time. His tanned face, which always gave off kindliness and strength, was pale and intent this time, and his eyes expressed a deep, stinging outrage that wouldn't leave his mind even for an instant.

Is that Jerusalem? Is that the city of God for which he'd yearned from his tiny hometown all those many days?

On winter evenings, when he sat with his aged father, Mattathias, him and his brothers great and small, before the burning hearth, he'd heard his father sing the praises of the capital of Israel, his eyes gleaming with joy and in his heart a wonderful dream woven of the splendid city of David. He was fourteen already and had never left Modi'in, his tiny hometown, but how great had his rejoicing been when his father pledged to send him this very spring to Jerusalem. Since then, all his wellsprings day and night had been set only on the Lord's city that sat over the mountains wreathed in blue—the city that was the glory of God and the glory of man both joined together. He was always aware, of course, that the Syrians, an alien people, were now ruling the country, but they'd drive them off one day like bad dogs from the mountain of Zion. The naive lad could not believe that Jerusalem, the royal city, which had the Lord's Temple in it, had become an all but Greek city, and that even his own relations, the family members of the High Priest, spoke the Greek jargon and mimicked the ways of their oppressors, not just out of necessity but of their own free will—to curry favor with the foreign rulers. Like one walking toward his joy without a word, Judah the son of Mattathias the Priest went to Jerusalem. Much had the lad heard from his father and elder brothers about the Greeks abusing the people of Israel and their rituals, but it was only now when he saw with his own eyes Jerusalem debased and desecrated that he felt the degradation of his people like the sting of a flame searing his heart. Just one day had he spent in Jerusalem. Nor had he seen the sights of all its precious things—he didn't want to see them. In this city, where even the priests' children prattled in a foreign jargon and were given foreign names, he saw himself a stranger in a strange land. For naught did he argue the wrong to his people and his God with the children of the rich priest among his cousins whose house he lodged in: they couldn't understand his language and mocked his simple clothes and small-town ways.

No, this was not the city his soul had longed for all those days and nights. It had once been the holy city, the visionary edge, perhaps once more it would be the most splendid Israel. But now it was nothing but a national disgrace, a city of flatterers and turncoats, whom he despised more than he hated the tyrannous Greeks. All night the youth denied his eyes sleep, all night he tossed and turned where he lay and groaned in pain and shame. And in the morning bright and early he rose and went alone up to the Temple Mount. There he stood in prayer a long while and shed hot tears over his pain and outrage; then he rose and left the city with a bitter heart, the same heart that had trembled with exhilaration just two days before.

II

HOW IT EASED HIS HEART to get down the mountains from Judea and breathe the air of the fields of Modi'in! The nearer he got to the little town, the more his eyes lit up. No, not there, in the city of a king, but rather here, in the small and humble town, was the faith in the God of Israel and his rituals still kept. From here, only from here, this honest soil, would the spirit grow that would eat like fire the slavery in which priests and dignitaries in the capital were mired up to their necks.

His hand slacked now from the donkey that made its way slowly to Mount Modi'in. You could already feel the sea tang in the air. Fields of wheat waved to the right and left of the way and groves of olives and grapes blossomed on all the slopes. The heart stilled suddenly and the pain seemed to ease. Here, yes—here was the motherland.

When he ascended the mountainside where Modi'in sits, the sea blinded his eyes with its foaming waves. A fierce wind gave the trees in gardens a spring shake. But he too, like a tender sapling, was given a merry springtime shake. He felt the earth of his own town beneath the sole of his foot, a land of rocks more powerful and precious than gold. From afar the coastal plain stretched out in the ruddy twilight glow. Sun-bronzed men came back from the field tired with drooping lids. But it was comfortable here after the din of the metropolis, and easy breathing this sea air, that braced the heart and calmed it.

III

INDEED, FOR MANY DAYS the memory of Hellenized Jerusalem engraved itself deeper and deeper in the youth's heart. His father's house with its simple, modest ways were sevenfold dearer to him now. And sevenfold dearer the sayings of the Lord that his father the priest taught him. The more the boy matured, the more he learned to respect the law of Israel whose basis was a humble heart, the honesty and mercy of man, in contrast to the law of the Greeks which preferred strength and diligence to a man's better qualities. The more his heart was distanced from the Greek beauty whose genius was for external improvement, the more he learned to appreciate the virtues of Israelite charm, which was more modest but deeper, and more spiritual. While still a tender lad Judah already understood how fierce the war would be with the alien culture and the shimmer of its finery that entertained and captivated people who did not look too deeply and could not tell the difference between lofty Israelite humility and the charms of exotic art.

But indeed Judah realized with each passing day how much his brothers were drawn to the alien enchantments. Not merely in Jerusalem where the Greek plague spread day by day, and the office of High Priest was sold to whoever betrayed and ratted most, but even in his own small town the evil had infected many locals. Ahh! It was no longer the humble Modi'in where the spirit of Israel had been preserved in its pure form. Even to this remote outpost the rot had already reached, and one house after another and one family after another turned their back on their people and their God.

Only this consolation remained to those who were loyal to their race, that in parallel to all those who broke the covenant and degraded their dignity and that of their people, day by day the number swelled whose love of their people and their law walked the cliff face of these times, strengthening as it went. With incomparable devotion, these remaining few defended the life of the nation, and what was acquired through dedication became not only dearer but also lodged deeper in the heart. In these difficult days, when their people fought for their life, for the very survival of their soul, the concepts of Judaism renewed in it and became embedded in their consciousness. And who knows? It may be that only this clash of the culture of Israel and its enemy made the people recognize the nature of its culture, its higher quality.

IV

REALLY, AMONG THESE PEOPLE, who were known as the pious, there were very few men of action—that is to say, men who did not think it was enough to be fond of Judaism, and even be ready to sacrifice their lives over it, but who were actually willing to get up and *do* something to defend it. From among these few Judah found himself even fewer friends, lads with fierce souls, who were waiting for the necessary moment to rise against the alien subjugation and break the yoke from the people's neck. This was the first seed from which a national army later sprung, freeing the nation from its oppressors, with Judah the Maccabee at its head.

This was no longer the delicate and pale-faced boy who returned broken-hearted from Jerusalem, but an impressively formed young man who captured the heart of anyone who laid eyes on him with the beauty of his appearance and courage of his heart, the honesty of his soul. Faithful in all things, attentive as a son, as a brother, as a friend, always willing to give his life for what was dear to him, he became for all who knew him the very symbol of devotion. He knew how to draw the people with the magic of his voice to follow him and gladly risk their lives for the sanctity of a notion. While he was still a lad, a miraculous quality was palpable in him, wherein strength and softness, charm and heroism met. And all his father's house knew he was framed for greatness. Force and generosity—he was graced with both in equal measure, and nature always bestows these two traits on the nation's chosen, the one through whom it will be redeemed.

In caves and crevices of rocks these lads would gather and train their hands for war, taking counsel, discussing how to save the people from the existential threat hanging over them. They well knew that slight was their strength next to the massive enemy, but this didn't weaken their hand. Rather the opposite: it was actually the recognition that it was down to them, the few, to whom the task of setting the people free had been given, that planted the courage and certainty in their heart. Was it possible wickedness would survive for all time? Would justice not finally yield victory?

V

THE DAY CAME WHEN JUDAH realized that the grain sack was full and it was time to move, lest he miss his time. By chance it happened that he and a handful of his fellows were in Jerusalem when the young army chief, Apollonius, set upon the quiet and unsuspecting inhabitants of the city on a Sabbath, killing many and looting their goods, taking their wives and children prisoner and turning their homes to heaps of ruins. With eyes full of tears and blood Judah saw the cruel Greeks abuse his brethren, but he could not deliver them. For naught he waited, for the townsmen to rise as one man against the enemy, for them to wrench the cobbles from the street and wreak vengeance on their oppressors. For naught he tried to stir them to acts of self-defense, in public or underground, and not bare their necks to the slaughter like a flock of sheep. Nobody stirred. Then Judah saw that from Jerusalem deliverance would not spring. And he and his friends left the city in secret. But this time he didn't go back to Modi'in either, but rather turned his face to the desert.

In the desert he breathed a sigh of relief. In the desert a people would rise who hated slavery as much as death. The desert became for many days his rocky redoubt. On dark nights his men went silently in the mountains from village to village and set the fire of rebellion throughout the land. They didn't call the citizens of cities, but rather the men of the field who did not yet know subjugation. And there came to Judah, from all corners of the people, men for whom the dignity of their people and liberty were dearer than their own lives. And the young hero organized them in tiny platoon after platoon, light as jungle cats and disappearing like nighttime phantoms from the eye of the beholder, who lurked behind every heavy boulder and inside every hidden cave for the enemy army, and devastated them, and no man could overtake them or discover their hiding place.

This was the first act of the inspired commander who always knew how to pick his moment and yield victories with his limited forces against the massive enemy. From the first step he struck fear in the confident foe's camp and set confusion among its warlords. From the first step he brought to the enemy's consciousness that it was at war with a people who had stirred to wreak vengeance for their God and avenge their desecrated dignity. Antiochia reeled before the

Hebrew commander whose extraordinary military tactics made naught of all their efforts. Truly he was not just an exalted leader, but also the nation's chosen. There was magic in the name of Judah the Maccabee, which cheered the spirit of the people and instilled faith in every heart, that here had arisen a redeemer and a deliverer.

1956

Dolls of the World

Joanna Rakoff

The move was scheduled for late June, but the calls started coming in April. My parents had retired. Their new home—three thousand miles away, a condo in a San Jose retirement community—was a fraction of the size of the house in which I'd mostly grown up. There would not be room for, say, a collection of evening gowns spanning the four decades of my parents' marriage—from a New Look-style red satin to a sleek, dolman-sleeved shift, loaded with linebacker sized shoulder pads—or an elaborate set of Waterford goblets, five-piece service for twelve, which would not have looked out of place on Edith Wharton's most formal table. In California, life would be casual. My mother would buy new clothes, new dishes, new furniture, all trimmed and modern. But before she did so, she needed to get rid of the old stuff, a lifetime's worth of anniversary presents and birthday presents and Mother's Day presents, of Nambe vases and silver-handled fruit knives and needlepoint renderings of Oriental style flowers, of fondue pots, iced-tea spoons, and toothpick holders, of Braun electric hand mixers, banquet-sized coffee percolators, and automatic foot massagers.

All of these things—and, of course, many more—had for years been neatly stowed in kitchen cabinets, in the rows and rows of built-in closets my mother installed in our massive basement, in the squat Ethan Allen buffet in our dining room. After Passover, my mother began removing them. And the phone calls began: Did I want the Balinese bark prints we'd picked up at Cost Plus when I was four? What about Grandma Pearl's love seat? The gallon-sized turquoise thermos we occasionally took to the lake? Those fondue pots? Twenty-four miniature cocktail forks carved out of ivory? The etched glass martini glasses my mother had registered for in 1951 but had never liked and had rarely used? The sheets I'd slept on as a young child, imprinted with a repeating image of Raggedy Ann and Andy at play? Or those I'd switched to at eight or nine, a Laura Ashley print of pink, nearly abstract rosebuds? The lamp in the family room with the pear shaped glass base?

Sure, I said, nervously, wondering where I would put all this stuff, wondering if I really wanted it. I was twenty-five and made $265 per week as an assistant at a literary agency. Most of my belongings came from the enormous Salvation Army in Astoria. It would be foolish to refuse anything, and yet, as my mother named thing after thing, I felt increasingly inclined to say no. I could not, somehow, imagine a future in which I gave dinner parties elaborate and large enough to necessitate several identical sets of crystal and silver salt and pepper shakers, after which my guests would lounge on my mother's cream-colored sofa, delicately sipping aperitifs from the smaller siblings of those maligned martini glasses. My mother sold the crystal, a souvenir from a trip to Ireland, for $15,000. I suggested that my sister might like the living room sofa.

The calls kept coming. At work, I swiveled on my chair and glanced at manuscripts as she listed the things she'd unearthed in the cedar closet. Years ago, when B. Altman's went out of business, I bought two glass plates—one for Amy and one for you—and I *completely* forgot about them. Oh, Joanna, they're *gorgeous*. Yours has a print of irises.

I've packed up your room, she told me in May.

I was planning on coming home and doing that, I told her, in carefully measured tones.

Well. I couldn't wait, she said. Anyway. And I've packed up some other silver odds and ends for you. The little candy dish. The fish trivet. But what about the menorah? I struggled to picture my parents' menorah. Was it brass? It hadn't figured prominently in my childhood mythology. Before I could answer, she said, You have Grandma's, right?

I had recently moved into my grandmother's apartment on the Lower East Side, which came equipped with a small, mildly confounding array of Judaica, including, actually, three different menorahs.

I do, I told her.

Okay, then I'm going to give ours to Amy. I think she lost hers in the move. This was a polite reference to both my sister's difficulty with maintaining ownership and upkeep of physical objects (including, but not limited to, her house, which had recently been covered in a volcanic spray of sewage, the result of neglecting their rural septic system for as many years as they'd lived in the place) and the fact that she'd recently left her husband and their three children—temporarily, we were told—and moved into a one bedroom apartment in Poughkeepsie, somehow misplacing various family objects on the five mile journey.

Sure, that sounds good, I told her. All I really want are the books. Whatever Amy wants is fine with me.

What Amy wanted, in the end, was most everything—or, at least all the big stuff—and this was, indeed, fine with me. Her house as it happened, was not actually hers. My parents, I'd just discovered, owned it. And they'd decided to sell it, to cut my sister—eighteen years my elder—and her husband off.

We're going to be on a fixed income, my father explained. We can't keep up that house anymore. We can't support them. They can save up and buy their own place.

An entire house worth of furniture wouldn't fit in my sister's little apartment, so my mother arranged for it to be transported to a storage facility nearby. And I, on a chilly night in early June, drove a dilapidated van out of the barbed wire-rimmed U-Haul lot on the Bowery, picked up the man who would, a few months later, become my husband, and drove upstate. The next day, I began slicing open box after box—my second bedroom was a sea of brown cardboard—and unfolding protective sheets of bubble wrap and newspaper and tissue. A white Wedgwood vase. Two copies of *The Joys of Yiddish*. A pewter pitcher with a pattern of vines snaking up and down its face. One grandmother's flatware, then another's. (My sister, I was told, had received yet another set.) The steel canister set—stamped sugar, flour, tea, coffee in the sans serif font popular in midcentury—that had sat on our kitchen counter, supplying the ingredients for hundreds of cookies and cakes and brownies. Worn wooden spoons. The painted glass lamp that had sat by my bedside through childhood. The green enamel pots my mother had bought when she moved into our old house, twenty miles south, in Nyack, a town I much preferred to our own. Four yellow pillowcases, never used, in a Marimekko-ish butterfly print. (Where were the matching sheets? I wondered.) A sari fabric dancing dress with a handkerchief hem. My beloved ice skates—Riedel silver stars and my skis and ski poles and ski boots, the latter still in the original box, with its stark black-and-white design. Linen tablecloths and damask tablecloths and cotton tablecloths embroidered with flowers. The heavy glass candy dish that had sat on the coffee table in our living room, the sole spot of color in my mother's palette. My parents' vast and wildly colored collection of liquor, which dated back to the earlier years of their marriage, when they entertained avidly: Chartreuse and Cherry Heering and Sabra and Blue Curaçao and Harveys Bristol Cream and Vandermint and amaretto.

By the time I came along, these bottles had been banished to a dark recess of the stereo cabinet, which ran along one side of our living room. Come Thanksgiving—when the extended network of Rakoffs and Avruts and Merlises and Senators tended to gather at our house—my father might pry the door open and, under the wary eye of my mother, gather the ingredients to make martinis for the various cousins who liked to hit the sauce. But at Chanukah, the cabinet remained firmly shut. Barring the occasional invitation to eat latkes at, say, the Siegels', we spent the holiday alone, with minimal to no merrymaking. Blue and silver wrapped presents were piled under and on top of the grand piano just north of the stereo cabinet; a blocky electric menorah was placed in the large front window. It was my job to twist the blue, ovoid bulbs into their sockets each night, as dark fell. Our real menorah—which was, yes, I was remembering, definitely brass—stayed in the kitchen, candles having been deemed too messy for the living room. Each night, before dinner and after lighting both menorahs, I sat in the dim, chilly room and quietly opened one gift, slitting the tape along the seams, just as my mother did.

Nearly twenty years later my habits hadn't much changed. As the day grew dark—and I grew sweatier, dustier, my hands darkened with newsprint—I found myself surrounded by a swarm of neatly opened boxes, their flaps yawning. There were things that were missing: the tall delicate pot that completed my Aunt Fritzi's chocolate set (not that I had any use for a chocolate set; not that I was even sure what a chocolate set *was*); a Mexican blouse, embroidered all over with flowers; a set of pastel portraits that had hung in our family room, that had probably—and deservedly—gone to my sister; and, most heartbreakingly, my dolls, which had sat, glassy eyed and squat legged, on the top tier of my white bookshelf for as long as I could remember. I'd expected to find them tucked into the corners of boxes, swaddled in stray pillowcases: the Russian peasant doll with real human hair; the china lady-doll with crumbling hoop skirt and parasol; the Japanese fabric doll, in elaborate kimono and obi; and, my favorite, the set of peachy-skinned, shiny-haired, plastic-bodied creatures known as Dolls of the World, which had played key roles in my multipart Barbie dramas. But there were no dolls to be found, save a battered rubber Kewpie in a faded orange dress.

When I creakily rose from the floor—ready to shower; not ready to find a place for the thousand objects I'd just unpacked—I saw I'd left one box unopened, a box labeled large silver. Once again, I pulled out the Swiss Army knife—itself a relic, survivor of umpteen summers at Camp Tel Yehudah, rescued from my dresser by my father—sliced open the packing tape, and began unwrapping soft, brown swathes of Pacific cloth. Serving pieces piled up around me, clattering on the worn parquet. There was the little candy dish—as a child, I'd filled it with halvah and jelly rings before company came—and the trivet shaped like a fish. The covered serving dishes, with their ornate curlicued handles, that had held boiled vegetables as recently as this last Passover. A set of small, tailored candlesticks. And then I found one last cloth bag, which contained something solid and heavy and large enough to fill the bottom of the box. The menorah, I thought for some reason, before remembering that no, that had gone to my sister. With weary hands, I pried the thing out and unzipped the bag. Inside was a round platter, with a solid center and a thick, filigreed edge, at the center of which was a lengthy inscription. It had, it seemed, been given to my mother by the Sisterhood of a synagogue called Sons of Israel to commemorate her five years of service as the president of said organization.

Sons of Israel? I thought. There were exactly three synagogues in the vicinity of the town in which I'd spent most of my childhood—the town we'd moved to when I was three; the town my parents would soon be leaving and none of them were called Sons of Israel. *President* of the *Sisterhood?* The mother I knew had no interest in religion—less than no interest. Her most potent memory from early childhood had to do with the tyranny of Orthodoxy: one of her aunts accidentally mixed up the milk silver and the meat silver; their father, her Grandfather Abraham, became so enraged that he threw both sets through the kitchen window. (*Through* the window, she liked to say. Not *out* the window.) When my father fondly recalled his own father's small shul on Norfolk Street, my mother said, Oh, come on. *Your father* took you out for shrimp chow mein on Saturdays. She was not, as far as I knew, a believer.

OUR TOWN WAS THE SORT of Jewish enclave that springs up, mysteriously, outside of New York—and, I suppose, D.C., Boston, and Chicago but my friends were not Rachel Weissman and Jillian Altchek. They were Sudha David, Zinnia Yoon, and Susan Conachey. At their houses I ate samosas and kimchi and, most remarkably, that cliché of clichés: anemic sandwiches consisting of one slice of bologna, another of American cheese, and two of white bread. None of this struck me as odd—or struck me at all, actually—until my eighth year, when the majority of my classmates began attending Hebrew school. Tuesday and Thursday afternoons, as the rest of Mrs. Cohen's third-grade class piled into cars, en route to Pomona Jewish Center (Conservative) or Temple Beth El (Reform) or Monsey Jewish Center (Conservadox), I boarded a near-empty bus back to Tamarack Lane, where I sat at the kitchen table and ate Danish butter cookies with my mother. That I preferred this activity to any other—certainly to any involving the other attendees of Lime Kiln Elementary School—made me vaguely uncomfortable, but I squelched such concerns with military-style force and retired to the family room, where, beneath those aforementioned portraits of beautiful, big-eyed children—the sort popular in the 1970s—that sat atop the Danish modern bookshelf, my vast collection of Barbie dolls served as actors in an elaborate saga involving a costume ball, a grandmother trapped in an attic, and a private production of *As You Like It* (a play within a play!), the précis of which I'd recently read in Charles and Mary Lamb's *Tales from Shakespeare*.

But come December, it became clear that something was very wrong. My Jewish classmates were, this year, talking about Chanukah in a new, enticing way. They were going to parties at which doughnuts were served and dreidels were spun and songs were sung and gifts were picked blind out of big bins. And they were also—how had I never noticed this?—recounting their families' celebrations, which involved grandmothers and aunts and uncles coming in from out of town and making big batches of latkes, and which reminded me of passages from one of my favorites series of books, Sydney Taylor's *All-of-a-Kind Family*, a chronicle of a big Jewish family on the Lower East Side at the turn of the century. The sisters—Ella and Henny and Sarah and Charlotte and Gertie—bought pickles and penny candy and ate them on their stoop, when they weren't curling their hair with hot tongs or making costumes for Purim or helping their mother prepare for Shabbes dinner. Even while dusting, these girls had fun—true, boisterous *fun* of a sort I'd never quite experienced, living, essentially, like an only child in our pale, quiet house—and it occurred to me that they, like my classmates, went to Hebrew school.

Cautiously, I broached the subject with my mother. She explained that to attend Hebrew school one had to belong to a synagogue, and we did not belong to a synagogue because my parents—my mother—didn't like any of the options. Pomona Jewish Center, she felt, was materialistic: their dues were unbelievably high, their members the sort of women who would soon come to be known as Jewish American Princesses (their children were my most popular, and poisonous, classmates).

Services at Temple Beth El were, she said, akin to going to church. Monsey Jewish Center was located dangerously close to the Hasidic neighborhood of New Square. Of this, my mother could only shake her head in horror.

The real problem, of course, lay not in the synagogues, with their various flaws, but in my parents' faith, or lack thereof.

We're not sure we believe in God, my mother finally explained.

Things have happened, my father chimed in, turning his face toward his shoes, as he did whenever difficult subjects (like my sister) arose, that made us think there might not be a God.

They were, I assumed, talking about the Holocaust. This made sense to me. I had read Anne Frank's *Diary of a Young Girl* and was working my way through every other Holocaust or World War II themed novel I could find at the library—and while I didn't begrudge Anne's right to believe, in spite of everything, that people are truly good at heart, it seemed to me, with my knowledge of her fate, that a

God might have allowed some wandering in the desert, some enslavement, some slaying of sons, but He or She would not, could not have stood for the attempted extermination of his allegedly chosen people. Oh, I told my father. Okay.

All of this went a ways toward explaining my family's interpretation of Chanukah, which struck me, by comparison, as rather like those bologna sandwiches Susan Conachey's mother served: thin, anemic. Not just because my parents didn't even feign an interest in Judah Maccabaeus, not just because no blessings were mumbled as we lit the candles, but because—and you have already guessed this, no doubt—they lacked the gaiety that I seemed, recently, to be hearing much about. Occasionally, latkes made an appearance on the holiday table, but only occasionally; my mother didn't love to cook, in general, and, in particular, disliked anything that made a big mess. Standing over a frying pan for the better part of an evening, getting splattered with an ever-graying batch of batter and hot spurts of corn oil, was definitely not on her list of favored tasks. But what baffled me was that while our family was large and mostly clustered in and around New York and Palo Alto, we never gathered at Chanukah, the way, it seemed, other families did. Even my sister was generally off doing, as my mother said, who knows what.

That year—my eighth year, the third grade—as the holiday was nearly upon us, my mother noticed that something was bothering me. I was quiet, reserved. She attributed this to feelings of alienation (though she didn't use that word) from the dominant culture of our nation. One night as I lay on my bed reading, she knocked on my door and came and sat down beside me. It's hard to be Jewish at Christmas, she said, in the low pitch she used for serious talks. Everyone is having fun. It's *seductive* . . . This word embarrassed me, with its sexual connotations (I had read Beverly Cleary's *Fifteen* and the entire Judy Blume oeuvre). It's *really* seductive. I know, trust me. The trees, the lights, the carols. It's beautiful. You want to be a part of it. I nodded and stuck my finger in my book. She must, I supposed, have been thinking of the tall fir in Susan Conachey's living room, or the Bing Crosby on the radio, which my father liked to sing along to, or the elaborate, buttery pastries we'd eaten a few nights back at the rustic home of some German immigrants, friends of friends.

But I, of course, didn't care about any of that. Christmas as practiced in contemporary America—the overly shiny ornaments, the illuminated Santas perched on rooftops, the synthetic red stockings with names inscribed in glitter—had little interest for me. The news reports of parents standing on line all night outside of Toys R Us to secure Atari consoles and Rubik's Cubes made me flush with shame. Worse still was the idea of compiling lists—of *asking* for what you wanted. But Christmas as it was lived in the books I read obsessively, over and over, filled me with a sick longing, rooted less in the specifics of religion, and more in the general ethos of the holiday, as embodied by various nineteenth-century novels, first and foremost Louisa May Alcott's *Little Women*.

What I wanted was a Chanukah as redolent of—as informed by—ingrained, unself-conscious tradition as the March girls' Christmas. I could imagine nothing better than to be a March girl—preferably my namesake, Jo (and in an alternate universe, in which she, not Amy, marries Laurie)—eating roasted chestnuts and donating my dinner to the poor family down the road and trading scrappy, heartfelt gifts, each chosen *specifically* for the intended recipient, with careful thought given to what she wanted, what she loved, what she might, in her heart of hearts, truly *need*.

But what *was* an authentic Chanukah for an American family? The truth is, there was no such thing. We grown-ups are now all too coolly aware of Chanukah's minimal religious significance, that it was a minor holiday, artificially boosted to Christmas-level status in the 1920s by a double-team effort on the part of Jewish leaders—who had watched the latest wave of Jewish immigrants rushing to partake of Christmas ("The purchase of Christmas gifts is one of the first things that proves one is no longer a greenhorn," a reporter asserted in the *Forward* in 1904)—and canny marketers, who began advertising their wares as ideal Chanukah gifts (and, in the case of Aunt Jemima flour, ingredients) in the then-booming Jewish press. Tellingly, the *All-of-a-Kind Family* books are filled with vivid descriptions of Purim and Passover and Sukkot but scarcely touch on Chanukah. My parents, born in the 1920s, had barely celebrated the holiday. My classmates, well, their parents were closer in age to my sister—they were baby boomers—and they were, in a way, the first generation to take for granted the import of the holiday as a consumer occasion and, to be fair, one for gathering family, Noel style, or, in my dream life, March-family style.

But I was not Jo March and, perhaps more important, my sister was no Meg March (though it occurs to me now that she bore certain similarities to *her* March namesake, the artistic, bratty Amy). For starters, she barely knew me. She'd left for art school soon after my birth but had quickly dropped out to marry, then divorce, a blond, mustached man with the improbable name of John Johnson and a charming tax-free business involving the sale of mood-altering chemicals. At my parents' behest—and with their financial backing, of course—she went to nursing school somewhere in the vicinity of our house, but she was rarely around. Throughout my childhood she would occasionally appear on our doorstep, her hair a different length or color—now choppy and short, one strand dyed blue; now tawny and long and permed—jumping furiously into my parents' arms, pouring herself one of my dad's Cokes, hunching tensely in an armchair while my father sat at the secretary in the living room and scrawled out a check for her, then racing off again in whatever little car she was driving at the time. I was always relieved to see her go, and ashamed of my relief.

Occasionally, her visits coincided with major holidays—and one year, my birthday—and this year, this eighth year, she would, it seemed, be around for Chanukah, or one night of it. In the spring, she would be getting married again (though we all pretended that her first marriage had never happened), this time to someone deemed acceptable by my parents: an X-ray technician and would-be doctor, Jewish, from Bricktown, New Jersey. His name was David and he liked to cook. This year, there would be latkes.

As Chanukah came closer, the gifts began to appear under the piano. Eight boxes of identical shape and size, with my name on each of them. This was unprecedented, and I was curious. On the first night, we lit the candles—my mother allowing me to hold the *shamash* by myself, for the first time—and the electric menorah; then my mother said, Are you ready to open a present?

Strangely, I felt nervous. What could be inside those identical boxes? Um, okay, I said.

She looked them over carefully, squinting at some incomprehensible marking in the corners, then handed me one. I think this one should be first.

Carefully, I peeled off the wrapping paper and found a thin cardboard box with a clear plastic window at the front. *Dolls of the World* it said, in black letters above the window. *Poland* it said below. Behind the window stood a small doll with honey-colored braids, a dirndl skirt, and a funny peaked cloth hat.

Wow, I said. Cool.

My mother beamed. I saw them and I just couldn't resist, she said. I would have loved these when I was your age. Amy had something like them, but they've disappeared, I think. Removed from the box, the Polish costumed doll blinked at me. I thought you should open Poland first, my mother explained, because—well, you know—your Grandma Pearl's family was from Warsaw. I nodded but felt deeply confused. My grandmother and her sisters all had deep black eyes and blue-black hair.

One by one, the dolls emerged: Spain, dark-haired, in a red-and-white polka-dot flamenco dress. Greece, with a black velvet vest and a wildly striped skirt. Italy, in a thin red, white, and green ensemble that seemed more a nod to the country's flag than its indigenous costumes. Being the diligent, dorky child I was, I brought each new doll into the family room and compared her dress to the portraits of native peoples in my *Encyclopedia Britannica* set. To my surprise, they appeared to be fairly accurate.

On the eighth night, my sister and David arrived, full of chatter about the wedding and my sister's new job, in a psych unit at Cornell Medical Center. I showed her my dolls, the last of which I'd just opened: Sweden. I was still dismayed by their physical characteristics: Why was it that the Spanish doll was the one that most resembled me, when our family had come from Russia and Poland?

Well, Polish people—actual Polish people—are generally fair, my mother said. And Jews can be from Poland, but they're still Jews. They don't look like Poles, usually. So maybe if there was an Israeli doll it would look like you. Or an American doll.

I nodded. Or a Jewish doll, I said confidently and was surprised when my mother laughed. I don't think they would make a *Jewish* doll, she said. It would be an Israeli doll.

My sister folded the dolls' legs and sat them in a row on the floor of the family room, as if they were watching television.

I can't remember if I still played with dolls when I was your age, she said. I was never that into them. I always wanted to play outside. I nodded solemnly. My mother had said the same thing. Amy had scars all over her legs from falling off roofs and out of trees, while I had to literally be pushed out my front door when the warm weather hit. But dolls are cool, she said. I love these dresses. They're really pretty.

I thought about asking her why there couldn't be a Jewish doll but instead found myself pointing to the pastel portraits on top of the bookcase.

Who are they? I asked. It had not occurred to me, until the words left my mouth, that they *were* anyone—anyone other than anonymous, beautiful faces, like the faces of princes and princesses in fairy tales. And as soon as I finished the sentence, I saw that this was the wrong question to ask—and also the right one. My sister's face had gone blank and slack.

You know who they are, she said.

No, I said. I don't.

You do, she insisted. I shook my head. Sighing, she pointed to the girl on the right, with dark hair and green eyes under thick brows. That's me, she said.

You! I almost shouted.

Yes, she said, and drew her lips in a thin line. And that's Anita—she pointed to the blond girl, my favorite of the three, with her shy, wide smile and kind eyes—and that's Mark. My brother and—*our* brother and sister.

I wasn't sure what to say, what else to ask. Suddenly, many things made sense. The questioning of God. The sudden sadness that came over my parents, like a summer storm. There was an accident, she said. I was there, too—and then she turned away. Mom and Dad can tell you, she said. They'll tell you when you're old enough. I nodded. I'm going to find David, she said. Okay? Okay, I said. Okay.

But it was never okay. They never told me. There was an accident, I knew, and my brother and sister had died. My sister, a cousin eventually revealed, had been in a coma for weeks or months—the cousin couldn't remember; it was a horrible time, he said—and awoke changed. She had brain damage? I asked. No, my cousin said. She couldn't live with the guilt. She was the one driving the car.

IN CALIFORNIA, MY PARENTS THRIVED. Our rapidly multiplying Palo Alto relatives, the cousins with whom my mother had been raised, like siblings, and their children and grandchildren—gathered weekly for potluck dinners and held big, unruly Seders. You would love it here, they told me. So would Evan. At our wedding, in October, they gave us a large, shiny brass menorah in a traditional style of interlocking arches. It was a grand-looking thing, and Evan—who preferred silver to brass, matte to shiny, modern to traditional—looked at it doubtfully, then tucked it in the linen closet, behind the million sheets and tablecloths I'd unpacked three months prior, and next to the monstrous silver platter, the origins of which I'd still not figured out. But in December, I pulled the menorah out and placed it on top of our piano, a mahogany baby grand with a cracked soundboard, inherited, along with the apartment, from my grandmother. Each night we lit the candles—I had learned the blessing as a teenager, at camp—and the glow, brighter each night, reflected back the warm sheen of the Wurlitzer, casting long shadows on our pristine walls. By the last night, Evan was won over. The menorah stayed on the piano through the new year, then moved to the old yellow bookcase in the foyer, the first thing visitors see when they enter our apartment—the first thing we see when we come home.

Exactly a year after their move, my parents returned to New York for a visit. For a few days they stayed with Evan and me on the Lower East Side—the vases and fruit knives and fondue pots they'd bequeathed us now neatly stashed in our crumbling kitchen—before heading upstate to visit with my sister, who had returned to her family. My sister and her husband had not, of course, been able to buy a new house—or even an apartment—and after a brief, disastrous stay in a friend's cottage (they'd flooded the place; the friend was suing), they'd moved into a residence motel, of sorts, with a two story medieval knight in its parking lot. My parents were not pleased. Amy's a blonde, my mother sighed, wearily, into the phone at the Poughkeepsie Holiday Inn (they'd dismissed the knight-guarded motel as sleazy; a fair assessment, I would soon discover). Not just a blonde, a *platinum* blonde.

That weekend, my husband and I drove up the Taconic and checked into the Holiday Inn. Moments later, my mother burst into our room, suggested that Evan play a round of golf with my father, and hustled me off on some invented errand. As soon as we hit Route 9, she said, It's all gone. Everything is gone.

I didn't understand. What's gone?

Everything, she said. Everything. She didn't make the payments on the storage facility. Not even one. They sent her three warnings, then they auctioned everything off.

You're kidding, I said, for this seemed a real possibility to me, more possible, somehow, than my sister's losing everything, the material sum of my parents' life together. (Later, when I told a close friend what had happened, she was shockingly nonplussed. Amy fucked up again, she said. Big surprise.)

I should have given you Grandma Pearl's love seat, my mother said.

And the menorah, I said. She gave me a funny look.

What menorah?

Our menorah, I said, with a hint of impatience.

I didn't give Amy our menorah, she said. What would Daddy and I use? *We* still need to the light candles, don't we? I assented that they did. I love that menorah, she said, with a smile. We've used it for years. And you know what's funny? I can't even remember where it came from. This was indeed funny, coming from a woman who could recall the provenance of every dress she'd ever placed on her back. Why would we give Amy our menorah? she asked again.

You said . . . I began, then stopped. What was the point? Then, suddenly, I remembered the portraits—the pastel portraits of Amy, Anita, and Mark. Had she given them to Amy? I felt slightly panicky at the thought of this. Hey, I said. What's Sons of Israel? I asked instead, surprising myself.

Sons of *Israel?* she said, all trace of laughter gone. It's the synagogue in Nyack. Why?

Nyack, our Nyack? Where we lived when I was a baby? She nodded. There's a platter. It was in one of the boxes you gave me. From the Sisterhood . . . Suddenly, I felt uncomfortable. This was not, I was sure, something she would want to talk about. Not now, certainly, but maybe not ever. And I had known this; this was why I'd waited so long to ask.

She nodded again and swallowed. We were founding members, she said. Back before you were born. Way back. Mark had his bar mitzvah there. Before the accident . . . I nodded quickly to cut her off. If you had asked me, at the time, I would have said I wanted to spare her the pain of talking about my brother and sister. But now I suppose it was a selfish move: I was terrified of what she might say. She went on anyway. Afterward, we just couldn't go back. With everyone feeling sorry for us. We were always reminded of them. Everywhere we looked. We had to move away.

For a moment, we sat, and then she unbuckled her seat belt and, with a grin, pointed to the T. J. Maxx. Should we go shopping? It seems like we deserve some new stuff.

Sure, I said.

As we walked across the cracked pavement, along the rows and rows of nearly identical cars, she put her arm around me and I remembered:

My dolls, I said. Amy had my dolls.

No, she didn't, my mother said quietly.

She *did*, I said, hating the slight whine that crept into my voice. I was supposed to be the strong child, the mature child, the wise child. I was the child of their old age, the child who would take care of everything, who would right all my sister's wrongs and replicate every joy of those I was conceived to replace. I was the child who never asked for anything. But I wanted my dolls. You accidentally gave them to her. Just like the butterfly sheets.

No, I *didn't*, she insisted, her voice rising, and I knew, for sure, that she was going to cry. We were approaching the sidewalk, the threshold of the store, where rack after rack of clothing awaited her gimlet eye, her expert knowledge of cut and drape and fabric and make. I would *never* give Amy your dolls. How could you say that? You loved those dolls. They were your *friends*.

But I didn't find . . .

I packed them away in a box, a ski box, a square box with a handle . . .

A *ski* box? I asked.

A ski *boot* box, she said. A Salomon box. Wasn't there a Salomon box?

There was, I told her, and guided her inside.

That night, we made an attempt to eat dinner together as a family at a steak house favored by my youngest nephew, then six. But my mother was furious and couldn't even look in the direction of my sister, who was indeed as blond as Madonna, with bangs like Sandra Dee's. After the waitress took our order, Amy began sobbing. My teenaged niece looked like she wanted to hide under the table. My brother-in-law pretended everything was fine. Eventually, Amy left the table and never came back. We spent the rest of the night searching for her. The next day, Evan and I drove home in silence, through a hot, heavy rain. In the front closet, on the highest shelf, next to my ice skates and Evan's basketball, I found the black-and-white box—I'd saved it, as a teen, because I'd liked the design—brought it into our bedroom, and opened it up. The dolls were packed in layers, like candy. I pulled out the Japanese lady, the china lady with her parasol, a black-haired flapper doll, the Russian doll, her wiry hair disintegrating. And there, below them, were the Dolls of the World, their bright costumes a tangle of rickrack and ribbons and wide-brimmed hats and black Mary Janes, their blue eyes still blinking, their cheeks still dewy and fresh, their hair still shiny and thick. One by one, I pulled them out—their plasticky scent still strong, still familiar after all these years—and read off the names of their countries, imprinted in gold on the bottoms of their shoes. Spain, Mexico, Holland, Poland, Greece, Italy, France, Sweden.

Hello, I said to them. Hello, I said.

You're still here, I said. You're home.

2007

Two Chanukah Lamps

S. Y. Agnon

There was a Chanukah lamp in the synagogue, made of tin, with the shape of the Temple on it, along with the Chanukah blessings and thanks for miracles. The well for each candle was wide and deep and its mouth was pulled outward. All year long it would hang on the northern wall, where they'd hang the matzoh to annul boundaries for Sabbath in the city, but on Chanukah evening the beadle would take it down, wash it, polish it, set it on the table opposite the door, put oil in it, take wicks, and that night he would light it.

One year near Chanukah the beadle wanted to arrange the Chanukah lamp for the nights of Chanukah but could not find it. He rummaged in all the usual places but could not find it. The affair was talked of all over town until the rumor came to the schoolchildren. The Almighty put it in the mind of all of them to give their dreidels up to make of them a lamp for Chanukah. Instantly they took their dreidels and brought them to the artisan and promised to give him his recompense—all the Chanukah gelt they'd be given by their fathers and family at Chanukah. It was not two or three days, and some say only one, before the artisan made them a lamp for Chanukah. The children took the lamp and brought it to the synagogue. At night they lit Chanukah candles in it.

Near Passover when they prepared the synagogue in honor of Passover they found the lost lamp lying under a bench. They took it and set it back in its place.

The next year the beadle wanted to light the Chanukah candles in it. The elders of the synagogue said that the children who gave up their dreidels and all their Chanukah gelt for a replacement lamp were worthy of lighting candles in that newer menorah. And so they arranged that they would light the lamp of lead made by the children even though the big lamp was handsomer. The light of the children would light year by year on the nights of Chanukah. But after the abomination of desolation came with his bevy of admirers impure and cursed, the light went out.

1965

This story was part of a collection called *A City in Its Fullness*, set in Agnon's birthplace of Buczacz in Polish Galicia where he lived until immigrating to Palestine in 1908. Agnon learned in 1943 that the Jews of Buczacz had been massacred.

Gifts of the Last Night

Rebecca Newberger Goldstein

That the winds had taken possession of Manhattan on this last night of Chanukah; that they were roaming the wide avenue, snarling and hissing like a pack of demons unloosed from Gehenna: This was not the way she would ever have described the situation. Pearl Pinsky had little use for metaphor and none at all for old-world hocus-pocus. The simple facts: It was late December, early dusk, and cold—damned cold, devilishly cold. Those winds.

Pearl had been waiting for almost an hour at her bus stop not far from Columbia University. Classes were suspended for the winter recess, and the neighborhood felt eerily emptied. She stood at this corner all by herself as the savage evening deepened around her into demented night. Her eyes—streaming cruelly from the cold behind her bifocals—were the lone eyes fixed on the dimming west, from where she expected momentarily to see those bright head beams rounding the corner from Riverside Drive. Meanwhile, it got only darker, and the imps of the air were whooping it up with the ends of the long woolen scarf Pearl was vainly attempting to keep wound across her face, breathing open-mouthed into the fuzzy wool to generate some warmth. It was an incongruous scarf to be seen on a middle-aged woman of an otherwise serious cast. Splattered with primary colors, it was like something a little child might have worn or perhaps even have painted. This was a woman who gave little thought to appearances.

At exactly the moment at which she had despaired of finding even a taxi on this lonely stretch of Broadway abandoned to godless gusts, she turned and noticed a little plain restaurant. Nothing fancy, nothing trendy. To say it was modest is already to overdo it. Not a glance of the brilliance of the festive season fell upon it. Not a single colored light bulb glimmered; not a glitter of a word had been hung to wish a patron or a passerby a merry this or a happy the other. Squeezed in as it was between the corner and a dazzlingly done up Gap store glowing with a white star and a sentimental message, a person might almost not have noticed it at all.

But Pearl had noticed. The winds themselves had taken hold and almost lifted her bodily from the pavement—she was, after all, not so much to lift, a short woman, full-figured, but still not weighing more than maybe 115 pounds—and had ungently nudged her through the door, slamming it shut behind her, so that all again was calm within the ill-lit establishment where a lone customer sat eating his applesauce.

He looked up, his spoon poised on its way to his open mouth and stared intently at the bedraggled female suddenly brought before his gaze: the intellectual high forehead, black-framed glasses, and slightly sagging jowls; the bulging book satchel, incongruous scarf, and unraveling skirt drooping from beneath her coat. He took note of all the telling details, but of the scarf most of all. He was a writer.

Her age, he guessed exactly—it was what she looked, and a woman who wore such a scarf would have taken no pains to disguise the truth. Years ago, when the writer had been a man in all his vigor, he used to feel a certain mild outrage with such a woman as this, who took so little care to acknowledge and augment the Feminine Principle within her. This had been a great theme for him, both in his work and in his life—namely, the Feminine Principle. With him, it had never simply been a matter of a love affair, of which he had had a not insignificant number. Rather, it had been more a matter of paying homage to the Feminine Principle wherever he had happened to find it realized and available in this or that particular lady of his acquaintance.

He had been born to a woman who had known even while he had not yet vacated her womb that her firstborn would be a boy child of remarkable genius destined to transform—at the least—the century. Nothing in his childhood had dimmed his mother's certainty, which had quite naturally been duplicated in him. The consequence was that he had been the sort of a man who couldn't feel the insistent urgings of his manhood without at the same time endowing them with universal themes and erecting them into a theory of art and of life. The exact details of this theory we can forget because even the writer had by now forgotten them. They had gone the way of the urgings, so that now he could examine this woman with nothing of his old outrage.

Tonight was the very last night of Chanukah. All evening he had been aquiver with anticipation, unable to suppress his sense that the universe was not altogether indifferent. It had been the tradition when he had been a boy that each successive night of Chanukah, his presents from his parents had gotten progressively more wonderful, a practice grounded in sound theology. After all, the ancient miracle of the little holy lamp that had continued to burn on such meager fuel—this miracle had gotten better and better with each passing day. The presents that it had been his to receive on those last nights of the magical Chanukahs of his childhood, these he could recall in loving detail until this day. When he had been five years old, he had received a tiny violin, sized just right for his little cheek and shoulder. When he had been six, it had been the entire set of the *Book of Knowledge* encyclopedias, all of whose twenty-five volumes, with appendix, he had read by the time he was eight. In fact, it had been of his beloved *Book of Knowledge*, with its many magnificent pages of full-color plates, that he had only now been thinking when the restaurant door was flung open and his attention diverted. So that when Pearl Pinsky returned her defogged bifocals to the bridge of her nose—not a bad nose, he had noted, though a little wide—she found an old man's watery, red-rimmed eyes avidly fixed upon her. By this time, the writer knew what he knew, and he closed his mouth around a smile as if he and this woman were on old familiar terms with each other.

"Do I know you?" asked Pearl.

"Such winds!" responded the writer with a sympathetic little shiver. "Snarling and hissing like a pack of demons unloosed from Gehenna."

"Gehenna!" The woman gave a short little hoot of a laugh. She had a high-pitched voice more girlishly sweet than he would have anticipated, with just a hint of the plaintive to curdle it.

Without any ceremony, she came over and sat herself down opposite the writer at his little Formica table against the wall.

"Gehenna!" she repeated as she placed her book bag on the floor between her feet. "I thought it was supposed to be hot in Gehenna."

"You thought wrong," the writer answered.

Pearl was inclined to hoot once again, but she only snorted and rather gently at that. The man across from her—palsied and bent, with only his imperious nose and vivid eyes still undiminished—was about the same age that her own father would have been, although her father would have had even less use than she for the quaint choice in metaphor just voiced. Simon Pinsky had been all sorts of things in his lifetime, including the editor of a Jewish anarchist newspaper, which had had its heyday when Pearl had been a child. She and her anarchist father had been comrades till the end, and Pearl had always felt most comfortable with men of Simon's generation.

"You know, it's a funny thing," she confided after she had given her order for tomato soup to the young waitress. "I wait at this corner almost every evening for my bus, and I never once noticed this restaurant."

"You're probably preoccupied. You strike me as a very preoccupied person." He stared at her for some moments more. "I wonder," he began slowly. "I wonder if you even realize what tonight is."

She looked at him blankly.

"It's the eighth night of Chanukah. The very last night—the best night!" He finished on a high note, almost a squeak, a spray of spittle punctuating his excitement.

"Well, you're right there," Pearl answered, frankly taken aback. The old man was leaning toward her, his striped tie in his applesauce, his eyes—protuberant to begin with—gazing into hers with strange meaning. "I mean, you're right that I wasn't aware."

"I knew it. I knew you had forgotten."

"It doesn't mean all that much to me."

"You think you have to tell me that? You think I can't figure that out for myself?" he demanded in an aggrieved tone. He sat back in a sulk.

"So why is the last night the best night?" Pearl asked him. Her father had also had a quirky temper, as had many of the men of his generation whom Pearl had known. She was an old pro when it came to this kind of appeasement. "I never heard that one," she threw in for good measure.

He didn't want to admit to her that the source of his pronouncement was only the order in which he had received his Chanukah presents as a boy. She was clearly a very intelligent woman. He wouldn't be surprised to learn that she was a lady professor. But still she was also just as clearly a person completely ignorant on the subject of Jewishness, so that he could lie to her if he wanted, which he did want.

"It's part of the religion," he said, and took another spoonful of his applesauce.

"So if this is the best night, you should at least have some potato latkes to go with that applesauce," she said smiling so girlishly sweet that he immediately repented.

"You know what, Ms.—"

"Pearl," said Pearl.

"Pearl, I have a little something for you." He reached down into his pants pocket, fumbling around until he pulled out a little black book, and handed it across the table to her. It was cheap imitation black leather embossed with gold Hebrew letters.

"It's a Jewish calendar," he said, smiling with the sudden pleasure of his own generosity. "Organizations are always sending them to me whether I send them back a donation or not. This one happens to be the nicest, but—I have others. Take it! It's hardly even used—one or two appointments I had in September. I penciled them in, but I'm not so much in demand as I used to be. It's almost as good as new, Pearl. And all the Jewish holidays they've got printed up, even the exact moment of the sunset when they start; this way, you'll at least know when you're not observing."

"Well, thank you," Pearl said her voice gone more girlish than ever. "Will you inscribe it for me?"

"With pleasure." He was, after all, a writer. It wasn't the first time in his life his autograph had been shyly requested. Women—young and old, married and single—used to flock when he had given readings, and then they would line up afterward to have him sign copies of his stories that they had clipped out from the Jewish newspapers. Pearl began to fish around in her purse for something to write with, but he quickly produced his own beautiful silver fountain pen, a gift he had received many years ago from one of his wealthier girlfriends.

"Chanukah, 1994," Pearl read. "With my best wishes on the last night. I. M. Feigenbaum."

Pearl looked up, her intelligent high forehead creased into wondering disbelief, her bifocals slipping down to the very tip of her short wide nose. "I. M. Feigenbaum. Are you *the* I. M. Feigenbaum, I. M. Feigenbaum the writer?"

"You know me?" the writer whispered, barely able to control his quivering voice. "You know me?"

Did Pearl Pinsky know I. M. Feigenbaum? And how she knew I. M. Feigenbaum! His brief heyday had coincided with the brief heyday of her father's paper, and sometimes Simon would receive a manuscript of a short story from the young author. Pearl's father had detested the writer I. M. Feigenbaum. It was not simply that this upstart was a sentimental bourgeois, whose writing did not even acknowledge the great class struggles of the day. It was far worse. His stories wallowed in superstition and obscenity, unnatural lusts alternating with old-world hocus-pocus, and Simon Pinsky had regarded each and every page from the pen of I. M. Feigenbaum as a profound and personal insult.

"Don't defile our trash cans with it," Simon Pinsky would command his wife, who helped out with the editing. "Our garbage is too good to be associated with it. Flush it down the toilet, Hannah."

Simon Pinsky—as radical as he had been in his politics—had also had an almost rabbinical aversion to vulgarity. To hear him utter such a word as "toilet" was painful for his wife and daughter. (A secret: Hannah Pinsky, an otherwise dutiful wife, had saved each and every one of those rejected manuscripts.) In any case, such was the effect that the writer I. M. Feigenbaum used to have on Simon Pinsky.

Pearl's was a forthrightly truthful personality. When she knew something, her procedure was to come right out and say it. It was in her nature, therefore, to explain precisely how it was that she came to know so well the name of I. M. Feigenbaum. But for once in her life, she held her tongue. Staring across the little Formica table at the trembling old man whose face was luminous with the wonder of this extravagant gift, Pearl Pinsky blessedly held her tongue.

S. Y. Agnon (1888–1970) was a Nobel Prize–winning writer and one of the principal voices of modern Hebrew literature. Born Shmuel Yosef Halevi Czaczkes in Buczacz, in what is now Ukraine, he moved at age nineteen to Palestine, where he made his literary debut with the story "Agunot." From Palestine, he moved to Germany and then back to Palestine after a fire in 1924 destroyed his home in Bad Homburg. His novels include *The Bridal Canopy* and *Only Yesterday*. With poet Nelly Sachs, he was the co-recipient of the 1966 Nobel Prize in Literature.

Sholom Aleichem (1859–1916), one of the fathers of modern Yiddish literature, was born Shalom Rabinovitz in Pereiaslav, in what is now Ukraine. He began his literary career writing in Hebrew and Russian and published his first work in Yiddish under his pen name in 1883. He went on to publish his fiction in newspapers as he moved from Kyiv to New York City to Geneva, as well as in books including *Stempenyu: A Jewish Novel* and *The Adventures of Menahem-Mendl*. In 1894, he published *Tevye the Dairyman*, which would be adapted seven decades later into the Broadway musical *Fiddler on the Roof*.

Caroline Deutsch (1846–?) was born in Namesto, in what is now Slovakia, into a German-speaking family. She began writing poetry at a young age. In Berlin, she worked at the *Jüdische Presse* and published novelettes in the *Volks-Zeitung*. In 1875, she moved to Hamburg and wrote for the *Hamburger Nachrichten*. She wrote the novels *Über Klippen* and *Ein edles Frauenleben*.

Leon Elbe (1879–1928), also known as Leon Bassein, is the author best known for the 1929 Yiddish children's book *Yingele Ringele*. A native of Minsk, he immigrated in 1905 to New York, where he went on to publish a number of political works and children's books. He was a translator of Edgar Allen Poe into Yiddish.

Jacob Fichman (1881–1958) was a poet and essayist. Born in Bălți in what is now Moldova, he lived in Berlin, Odessa, Warsaw, and Vilna before settling permanently in 1919 in Palestine. He wrote in Hebrew and was the author of the poetry collection *Peat Sadeh* (A Corner of a Field) and the essay collection *Bavu'ot* (Reflections), as well as an editor of the journals *Moledet*, *Ma'abarot*, *Ha-Shilo'ah*, and *Moznayim*. His work was recognized with the Bialik Prize and the Israel Prize for Literature.

David Frischmann (1859–1922) was a writer, poet, and translator who is considered one of the first major writers in modern Hebrew literature. Born in Zgierz, Poland, he published his first writings and translations at the age of fifteen. For a few years, he lived in Berlin, where he translated from and wrote in German, as well as in Warsaw, where he wrote in Yiddish. He served stints as editor for *Ha-Dor, Ha-Zeman, Ha-Boker, Reshafim*, and the publishing house Stybel, first in Moscow and then in Warsaw.

Rebecca Newberger Goldstein (1950–) is a writer and philosopher whose books include the novel *The Mind-Body Problem* and the nonfiction work *Plato at the Googleplex*. Born in White Plains, New York, she has written biographical studies of Spinoza and the logician Kurt Gödel, has taught at universities including Brandeis and Columbia, and is the recipient of MacArthur and Guggenheim fellowships, the National Humanities Medal, and the National Jewish Book Award, among other honors.

Emma Green (1989–) is a journalist and staff writer at *The New Yorker*, where she writes about education and academia. Previously, she was a staff writer for *The Atlantic* covering politics, policy, and religion and managing editor for the magazine's website. She has received numerous awards from the Religion News Association, along with the 2020 Hunt Prize in Journalism, Arts, and Letters.

Gila Green (1970–) is a writer, editor, and English as a Foreign Language teacher. Born in Ottawa to an Ashkenazi-Canadian mother and a Yemenite-Israeli father, she has published the novels *White Zion, Passport Control*, and *King of the Class*, and the young adult novel *No Entry*. She lives in Israel.

Theodor Herzl (1860–1904) was a journalist and playwright, and the founder of the political form of Zionism. Born in Pest, Hungary, he was the Paris correspondent for the Viennese *Neue Freie Presse* during the Dreyfus affair, which had a profound effect on his later politics. In 1896, he published the pamphlet *The Jewish State*, which is considered a foundational text for modern Zionism, and in 1897 he was elected the first president of the World Zionist Organization at the First Zionist Congress. He died forty years before the establishment of the State of Israel.

B. Kovner (1874–1974) was the pen name of the poet, playwright, and humorist Jacob Adler. Born in Dynów in what is now Poland, he immigrated in 1892 to the United States, where he apprenticed as a tailor and worked in a factory. In 1911, he joined the staff of the *Jewish Daily Forward*; he also edited the *Brownsville Progress*, *Traumen un Wirklichkeit*, and *Der Yiddisher Gazlen*. Over the course of his career, he published over 18,000 poems, 30,000 humorous articles, and a dozen books.

Emma Lazarus (1849–1887) was a poet and essayist best known for writing "The New Colossus," the sonnet excerpted in an inscription at the base of the Statue of Liberty. Born in New York City, she published her first book, *Poems and Translations*, in 1867. It attracted the attention of Ralph Waldo Emerson, who would go on to become a mentor. By 1881, she had begun defending Russian immigrants' rights and protesting antisemitism in the pages of magazines such as *The Century*. She wrote "The New Colossus" in 1883.

Curt Leviant (1932–) is a novelist and translator. Born in Vienna, he arrived in the United States as a young boy. His interest in Yiddish took root early, and while in graduate school, he began translating Yiddish writer Lamed Shapiro. He has also translated works by Sholom Aleichem, Chaim Grade, and Isaac Bashevis Singer. The author of novels such as *Diary of an Adulterous Woman* and *Kafka's Son*, he has been recognized by the National Endowment for the Arts, the Rockefeller Foundation, and the Jerusalem Foundation.

Mendele Moykher-Sforim (1835–1917) was a foundational writer of modern Yiddish and Hebrew literature. He was born Sholem Yankev Abramovitsh in Kapyl, in what is now Belarus, and began writing fiction in Hebrew after leaving Kapyl for Ukraine as a young adult. In 1864, he published his first story in Yiddish, adopting the pseudonym by which he is now known. His novels in Hebrew include *Ha-Avot ve-Ha-Banim* (Fathers and Sons); his novels in Yiddish include *The Travels and Adventures of Benjamin the Third* and *Fishke the Lame*, which he later rewrote in Hebrew.

I. L. Peretz (1852–1915) was a poet, fiction writer, playwright, and lawyer. Born in Zamość, Poland, he practiced law for ten years and began his literary career writing in Hebrew and Polish, but soon switched to Yiddish. His first published Yiddish work, the ballad *Monish*, appeared in a journal edited by Sholom Aleichem. He moved to Warsaw after Imperial Russian authorities revoked his law license; in Warsaw, his home became a gathering place for young Yiddish writers. He was the publisher of *Yontev Bletekh* and the editor of *Di Yidishe Bibliotek*.

Chaim Potok (1929–2002) was a rabbi and writer. He was born Herman Harold Potok in Brooklyn, New York, and was ordained a Conservative rabbi in 1954. After serving as a U.S. Army chaplain in South Korea, he became managing editor of *Conservative Judaism* and the editor-in-chief of the Jewish Publication Society of America. His first novel, *The Chosen*, was published in 1967 and later turned into a film and a play; it was followed by the sequel *The Promise* and other novels.

Joanna Rakoff (1972–) is a memoirist and novelist. Born in Nyack, New York, she is the author of the novel *A Fortunate Age* and *My Salinger Year*, a memoir chronicling her time working for J. D. Salinger's literary agency that was turned into the 2020 film of the same name. The recipient of the Goldberg Prize for Fiction and the Elle Readers' Prize, she has taught at Columbia University and Brooklyn College.

Esther J. Ruskay (1857–1907) was a writer and speaker. Born in New York City, she was an accomplished orator and was the first woman to speak from the pulpit of New York's Temple Emanu-El synagogue. Her writing on Jewish life was published in a number of newspapers and collected in the 1902 *Hearth and Home Essays*.

Mark Strand (1934–2014) was a poet, essayist, and translator. Born in Summerside, Canada, he spent much of his formative years in the United States, Colombia, Mexico, and Peru. His work was recognized with a Pulitzer Prize (for his collection *Blizzard of One*), a MacArthur Fellowship, and three grants from the National Endowment for the Arts, and he was poet laureate of the United States from 1990 to 1991. Trained as a painter, he set aside poetry in his final years to return to visual art.

Elie Wiesel (1928–2016) was a writer best known for his literary accounts of surviving the Holocaust. Born in Sighet, in what is now Romania, Wiesel and his family were deported to Auschwitz in 1944; only he and his two older sisters survived. After being liberated in 1945, he was taken to Paris, where he studied at the Sorbonne and wrote for French and Israeli newspapers. In 1956, the same year he left for the United States, he published the memoir *And the World Remained Silent* in Yiddish, then rewrote a shorter version in French that was published as *Night*. He was recognized with the 1986 Nobel Peace Prize for "being a messenger to mankind [...] of peace, atonement and dignity."

A. B. Yehoshua (1936–2022), an Israeli writer and playwright, was born Avraham Gabriel Yehoshua in Jerusalem. After serving in the Israeli army, he began writing fiction, publishing his first book *The Death of the Old Man* in 1962. He taught comparative literature at the University of Haifa starting in 1972. His novels include *The Lover*, *A Late Divorce*, and *Mr. Mani*, and he was the recipient of the Bialik Prize, the Israel Prize for Literature, the National Jewish Book Award, the Dan David Prize, and other awards.

"The Chanukah Light"
Translated from the Yiddish by Helena Frank

"Judah the Maccabee" and *"Two Chanukah Lamps"*
Translated from the Hebrew by Atar J. Hadari

"The Last Hour"
Translated from the Yiddish by Abraham M. Klein

"Lighting Chanukah Candles in Death's Kingdom"
Translated from the Yiddish by Myra Mniewski and Chana Pollack

Excerpt from the novel *Friendly Fire*
Translated from the Hebrew by Stuart Schoffman

"To Grandpa's House for Latkes" and *"His Wife, His Latkes, and His Friend Peysekh-Moyshe"*
Translated from the Yiddish by Sebastian Z. Schulman

"Chanukah Money"
Translated from the Yiddish by Aliza Shevrin

"What's the Meaning of Chanukah?"
Translated from the Yiddish by Ri J. Turner

"The Miraculous Oil"
Translator unknown

"The Menorah"
Translated from the German by Harry Zohn

A VERY MEXICAN CHRISTMAS

A Very Mexican Christmas is sure to delight, warm, and astonish by turns. You'll find spellbinding work by some of Mexico's most important writers, including Carlos Fuentes, bestselling Laura Esquivel, and other contemporary favorites like Amparo Dávila, Sandra Cisneros, Fabio Morábito, and Carmen Boullosa, as well as fresh translations of classics by Sor Juana Inés de la Cruz, Amado Nervo, and Ignacio Manuel Altamirano.

A VERY GERMAN CHRISTMAS

This collection brings together traditional and contemporary holiday stories from Austria, Switzerland and Germany. You'll find classic works by the Brothers Grimm, Johann Wolfgang von Goethe, Heinrich Heine, Thomas Mann, Rainer Maria Rilke, Hermann Hesse, Joseph Roth and Arthur Schnitzler, as well as more recent tales by writers like Heinrich Böll, Peter Stamm and Martin Suter.

A VERY SCANDINAVIAN CHRISTMAS

The best Scandinavian holiday stories including classics by Hans Christian Andersen, Nobel Prize winner Selma Lagerlöf, August Strindberg as well as popular Norwegian author Karl Ove Knausgaard. These Nordic tales—coming from the very region where much traditional Christmas imagery originates—convey a festive spirit laden with lingonberries, elks, gnomes and aquavit in abundance. A smorgasbord of unexpected literary gifts sure to provide plenty of pleasure and *hygge*, that specifically Scandinavian blend of coziness and contentment.

A VERY FRENCH CHRISTMAS

A continuation of the very popular Very Christmas Series, this collection brings together the best French Christmas stories of all time in an elegant and vibrant collection featuring classics by Guy de Maupassant and Alphonse Daudet, plus stories by the esteemed twentieth century author Irène Némirovsky and contemporary writers Dominique Fabre and Jean-Philippe Blondel. With a holiday spirit conveyed through sparkling Paris streets, opulent feasts, wandering orphans, flickering desire, and more than a little wine, this collection proves that the French have mastered Christmas.

A VERY ITALIAN CHRISTMAS

This volume brings together the best Italian Christmas stories of all time in a fascinating collection featuring classic tales and contemporary works. With writing that dates from the Renaissance to the present day, from Boccaccio to Pirandello, as well as Anna Maria Ortese, Natalia Ginzburg and Nobel laureate Grazia Deledda, this choice selection delights and intrigues. Like everything the Italians do, this is Christmas with its very own verve and flair, the perfect literary complement to a *Buon Natale italiano*.

A VERY RUSSIAN CHRISTMAS

This is Russian Christmas celebrated in supreme pleasure and pain by the greatest of writers, from Dostoevsky and Tolstoy to Chekhov and Teffi. The dozen stories in this collection will satisfy every reader, and with their wit, humor, and tenderness, packed full of sentimental songs, footmen, whirling winds, solitary nights, snow drifts, and hopeful children, the collection proves that Nobody Does Christmas Like the Russians.

A VERY IRISH CHRISTMAS

This collection transports readers to the Emerald Isle with stories and poems sure to bring holiday cheer. The anthology is packed with beloved classics, forgotten treasures, and modern masterpieces. You'll find wondrous works by James Joyce, Elizabeth Bowen, W. B. Yeats, Anne Enright, William Trevor, Colm Tóibín, Bernard MacLaverty and many more.

AND THE BRIDE CLOSED THE DOOR by Ronit Matalon

A young bride shuts herself up in a bedroom on her wedding day, refusing to get married. In this moving and humorous look at contemporary Israel and the chaotic ups and downs of love everywhere, her family gathers outside the locked door, not knowing what to do. The only communication they receive from behind the door are scribbled notes, one of them a cryptic poem about a prodigal daughter returning home. The harder they try to reach the defiant woman, the more the despairing groom is convinced that her refusal should be respected. But what, exactly, ought to be respected? Is this merely a case of cold feet?

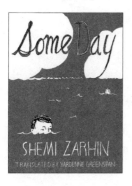

SOME DAY by Shemi Zarhin

On the shores of Israel's Sea of Galilee lies the city of Tiberias, a place bursting with sexuality and longing for love. The air is saturated with smells of cooking and passion. Some Day is a gripping family saga, a sensual and emotional feast that plays out over decades. This is an enchanting tale about tragic fates that disrupt families and break our hearts. Zarhin's hypnotic writing renders a painfully delicious vision of individual lives behind Israel's larger national story.

ALEXANDRIAN SUMMER by Yitzhak Gormezano Goren

This is the story of two Jewish families living their frenzied last days in the doomed cosmopolitan social whirl of Alexandria just before fleeing Egypt for Israel in 1951. The conventions of the Egyptian upper-middle class are laid bare in this dazzling novel, which exposes sexual hypocrisies and portrays a vanished polyglot world of horse racing, seaside promenades and nightclubs.

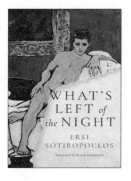

WHAT'S LEFT OF THE NIGHT by Ersi Sotiropoulos

Constantine Cavafy arrives in Paris in 1897 on a trip that will deeply shape his future and push him toward his poetic inclination. With this lyrical novel, tinged with an hallucinatory eroticism that unfolds over three unforgettable days, celebrated Greek author Ersi Sotiropoulos depicts Cavafy in the midst of a journey of self-discovery across a continent on the brink of massive change. A stunning portrait of a budding author—before he became C.P. Cavafy, one of the 20th century's greatest poets—that illuminates the complex relationship of art, life, and the erotic desires that trigger creativity.

THE 6:41 TO PARIS by Jean-Philippe Blondel

Cécile, a stylish 47-year-old, has spent the weekend visiting her parents outside Paris. By Monday morning, she's exhausted. These trips back home are stressful and she settles into a train compartment with an empty seat beside her. But it's soon occupied by a man she recognizes as Philippe Leduc, with whom she had a passionate affair that ended in her brutal humiliation 30 years ago. In the fraught hour and a half that ensues, Cécile and Philippe hurtle towards the French capital in a psychological thriller about the pain and promise of past romance.

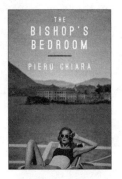

THE BISHOP'S BEDROOM by Piero Chiara

World War Two has just come to an end and there's a yearning for renewal. A man in his thirties is sailing on Lake Maggiore in northern Italy, hoping to put off the inevitable return to work. Dropping anchor in a small, fashionable port, he meets the enigmatic owner of a nearby villa. The two form an uneasy bond, recognizing in each other a shared taste for idling and erotic adventure. A sultry, stylish psychological thriller executed with supreme literary finesse.

THE EYE by Philippe Costamagna

It's a rare and secret profession, comprising a few dozen people around the world equipped with a mysterious mixture of knowledge and innate sensibility. Summoned to Swiss bank vaults, Fifth Avenue apartments, and Tokyo storerooms, they are entrusted by collectors, dealers, and museums to decide if a coveted picture is real or fake and to determine if it was painted by Leonardo da Vinci or Raphael. The Eye lifts the veil on the rarified world of connoisseurs devoted to the authentication and discovery of Old Master artworks.

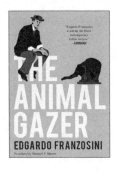

THE ANIMAL GAZER by Edgardo Franzosini

A hypnotic novel inspired by the strange and fascinating life of sculptor Rembrandt Bugatti, brother of the fabled automaker. Bugatti obsessively observes and sculpts the baboons, giraffes, and panthers in European zoos, finding empathy with their plight and identifying with their life in captivity. Rembrandt Bugatti's work, now being rediscovered, is displayed in major art museums around the world and routinely fetches large sums at auction. Edgardo Franzosini recreates the young artist's life with intense lyricism, passion, and sensitivity.

ALLMEN AND THE DRAGONFLIES by Martin Suter

Johann Friedrich von Allmen has exhausted his family fortune by living in Old World grandeur despite present-day financial constraints. Forced to downscale, Allmen inhabits the garden house of his former Zurich estate, attended by his Guatemalan butler, Carlos. This is the first of a series of humorous, fast-paced detective novels devoted to a memorable gentleman thief. A thrilling art heist escapade infused with European high culture and luxury that doesn't shy away from the darker side of human nature.

New Vessel Press

To purchase these titles and for more information please visit newvesselpress.com.